Freya peeked from behind the table. She never saw the gunman who approached her from behind.

But Stone did.

The moment froze as he weighed his options. He dropped to the floor and hurled himself past the men who were firing on him, taking two of them out as he passed. Stone focused on the gunman who was aiming at Freya. There was no way he could reach Freya or the gunman in time.

As if in slow motion, Stone saw the gunman lift his rifle to his shoulder and pull the trigger. The bullet spiraled towards Freya's head. Stone knew that while she was uncentered, she could not move out of the way quickly enough.

LEGACY

BOOK IV:
TRIAL AND TERROR

By Warren Murphy & Gerald Welch

This is a work of fiction. All characters and events portrayed in this novel are either products of the authors' overactive imaginations or are used fictitiously.

LEGACY, Book IV: Trial and Terror

By Warren Murphy and Gerald Welch

© 2014 Warren Murphy, All Rights Reserved.

ISBN-13: 978-0-9906566-3-0 (Destroyer Books)
ISBN-10: 0990656632

Requests for reproduction or interviews should be directed to: destroyerbooks@gmail.com

Official website: www.facebook.com/LegacyBookSeries

Cover and other artwork by Gerald Welch

Published by Destroyer Books/Warren Murphy Media
Edited by Devin Murphy

First public printing: November 2014
Printed in the United States of America

For Sarah, the indefatigable.

— Warren Murphy

To Leo Aromaa, who cost me five dollars.
To Tomas Gonzalez, for giving the world a Tomas,
And to Rob Tankersley, wherever you are.

— Jerry Welch

THE ISLAND NATION OF NAURU

Marcus Eames was four years old when he knew that he wanted to be a spy. Throughout his childhood, he filled his spare time with spy movies, spy books and detective training manuals. While his friends dreamed of becoming astronauts and firemen, Marcus told them that one day, he would become the world's greatest spy.

His home of Nauru was a tiny island nation barely outside the political influence of Australia. Though small, Nauru was wealthy; its citizens enjoyed the highest per-capita income in the world due to the nation's abundance of phosphates. These came from coral rock, limestone, and Nauru's vast abundance of seabird and bat guano. The droppings were so rich in minerals and other nutrients that they were prized the world over as the finest fertilizer money could buy.

Marcus's father was a man grounded in reality. The strip mining operations were producing fewer phosphates each year, so he began taking a large portion of his yearly earnings to set aside for his family's future. He knew of Marcus's desire to become a spy, but continually tried to dissuade his son from the silly notion.

"Nauru has no military, and certainly no spies," he told Marcus after his son had turned nine. "Your mother and I have sacrificed so that you can earn a comfortable living when the money from phosphates is gone."

Marcus's mother stood quietly in the background as she always had, lending silent support to her husband.

"I want to become a spy!" Marcus explained, his eyes wide with excitement.

"Marcus, that is a silly goal. You are becoming too old for this fantasy," his father said. "You should use your energy to become something sensible, like a doctor or lawyer."

"But I wish to become a spy," Marcus replied. "And my teacher says that we can always achieve our goals if we work hard enough."

His father grabbed Marcus by the shoulders and squeezed so hard that tears burst from his eyes.

"Your teacher fills your head with nonsense!"

"But father..." Marcus started.

"What country would accept a foreign spy?" his father yelled. "Do you really think that Australia or New Zealand would allow a foreigner access to their greatest secrets?"

"No, father, but America will," Marcus replied, hope beaming from his face. "In America, you can become whatever you wish to be!"

"Is this more stupidity from your teacher, or do you just watch too much television?" his father shouted, pulling Marcus closer until they were eye-to-eye. "Do you know what a spy's life is like? Hiding in fear that one day you will be found, always looking over your shoulder lest someone kill you."

"That is why I must study very hard," Marcus said. "I shall train my mind and body into a perfect weapon."

His father slapped Marcus to the ground. "Just who do you think you are? Do you think you're better than me? You will never become a spy!" he shouted.

Marcus's father grabbed his mother by the shoulder and they locked him in his room. Marcus never spoke of his dream to his parents again. He realized that if he was to become a spy, he could not count on their support.

He began by making a list of all of the skills he would need in order to be a great spy. He checked out every book the library had on becoming a detective, on foreign languages, and on martial arts. He wanted to be Sherlock Holmes and Batman all rolled up in one.

During his junior year of high school, he found a dusty volume in the back of the Nauru library entitled *The Way of the Sinanju*. The dusty tome was written by a nineteenth-century monk who had followed a Master of Sinanju for the duration of the Master's service to his prince. The monk noted with great detail everything he could about the Master.

The book was written as a historical account of the Master of Sinanju's great prowess in martial arts, but some of the things mentioned seemed too fantastic to be true. According to the book, Masters of Sinanju were able to perform impossible feats, such as dodging bullets and twisting steel with their hands. The book told of the unarmed Master walking into an ambush. Four men had hidden in the windows above with rifles. Shots rang out, but every bullet missed its mark. The monk noted with great care that the men were crack shots, and insisted that the Master was able to dodge the bullets due to his diet and breathing patterns. It was a very interesting read, but what captured Marcus's attention was the way the monk said that a Master of Sinanju observed things.

A Master of Sinanju did not lazily allow information to enter his mind. He sought out details of each new environment he entered. It was not the passive observation that humanity allowed. It was an active scrutiny that scoured the Master's surroundings for information. It began with changing the way you look at things—to have an active mind, controlling the things you noticed, rather than reacting to things as you came about them. Marcus began practicing immediately, and soon his mind became capable of remembering details most people would have immediately forgotten, or never have noticed in the first place.

His keen powers of examination allowed him to detect when people were a threat by how they moved. He knew when they were lying, when they were telling the truth, and when they would strike—giving him a keen edge in his martial-arts classes. Using the Sinanju techniques of observation, he could predict, with a startling accuracy, what move an opponent would make, often before they were able to realize it themselves.

The final chapter of the book was dedicated to the rare Sinanju ceremony of 'Sawon Ahm,' a blood oath between Sinanju and its client. The prince was so honored by the Master that he doubled the tribute. After Sawon Ahm, the Master would be prohibited from ever working for the prince again, but the treaty assured that Sinanju would not be hired to attack the nation during the life of the prince. Sawon Ahm could only be voided if the client attacked the Master or peoples of Sinanju.

Marcus pored over the book, absorbing as much information as he possibly could before beginning to read it yet again. He mimicked the Master of Sinanju's dietary restrictions and breathing meditations that the monk had recorded, but, to his immense disappointment, he still found himself unable to duplicate the Master's superhuman actions. While the monk had written prolifically about each detail he witnessed, several key details were obviously missing.

Marcus's days were filled with studies of political science and criminal psychology at the University of Melbourne. His nights were filled with foreign language tutoring, martial arts lessons, and, of course, his continual personal studies of the book *The Way of the Sinanju*. Marcus's knowledge of observation techniques allowed him to sail through his studies. His professors marveled at his ability to give detailed explanations for things he had barely seen.

As a freshman and sophomore, Marcus was at top of his class. He was on track to be at the top of his junior class until one evening, when he received a devastating call from Nauru's Chief of Police. His parents had been abducted.

They had left no note, and there were no signs of foul play. They had, as the Chief said, simply "gone up in smoke." Marcus, to his professors' vast disappointment, took an indefinite leave from his studies and returned home to his small island nation.

His parents' clothing, luggage, and passports were still in their home. The small jewelry box containing everything of value that his mother owned was still sitting on her dresser. Their bank account was untouched.

Despite round-the-clock work on the case, the small Nauru police force was able to generate no leads and uncover no clues. Their interest soon dwindled, and within two weeks, the police had stopped their investigation.

Marcus knew that if his parents were still alive, he would have to find them himself.

He continued the hunt for his parents, contacting everyone his parents had ever known. He traveled around his part of the world, searching for information, but it seemed that no one knew what had happened to the Eames couple. Some were more reluctant to talk than others, and although the people he talked to had all promised Marcus that they would contact him immediately if they heard anything, they never called. Many of them, Marcus sensed, went out of their way to give him intentionally wrong information, but Marcus never gave up his search.

Finally, four years after his search began, someone was willing to talk, and Marcus received his first real lead. A friend of his father's from decades ago claimed to have seen them in Saraburi, a small town north of Bangkok, Thailand.

Instead of wasting money on a wild goose chase, Marcus put his talents to work. Saraburi had no street cameras, but it did have an ATM. It was not difficult for Marcus to hack into the camera system, though it took several days to sift through the tens of thousands of grainy images stored in the ATM.

Marcus had been scanning pictures for days when he saw the first photo of his father. The man in the image was barely recognizable. A long, scraggly beard and unkempt hair hid most of his features, but the mole over his eyebrow was as distinct and recognizable as a fingerprint. His father had obviously spent a considerable amount of time in the sun. Deep wrinkles were carved his father's forehead where none had been before. Nothing of his father's former clean-cut image remained, but yet it was clearly his father.

The face of the woman beside him was mostly out of the frame of the picture, but he could still tell that it was his mother.

Marcus looked closely at the picture of his parents. They did not look as if they were in danger or worried about their only child. It looked as though they were a happy couple on vacation.

Emptying the last of the money from his trust fund, Marcus traveled to Thailand and took almost as many boats as cars to get to Saraburi. After three days of searching, he found his father at a local market. The man Marcus was trailing was no longer the confident man that he remembered. His father still possessed a powerful frame, but his face was gaunt and his hair had become thin, gray, and patchy in the back. He looked much older than his years. And then, when Marcus approached him, he ran as if he had seen the Devil himself.

Marcus gave chase. What possible terror could make a father flee from his only child? Marcus cut off his father before he reached his car, but as he went to greet him, his father struck him hard in the side of the head, knocking Marcus to the ground.

"You idiot!" his father screeched.

"Father, why did you hit me?" Marcus asked, staggering to his feet. "Why did you leave me?" he asked, his voice cracking.

"You should never have left Nauru! You were safe there!"

"Safe from what? From spies...spies like you, father?"

Marcus's father was stunned. His mouth flopped open uselessly before he was able to find words. "Like me? How did you know? We never said a word!"

"At first, I thought you and mother had an accident. But when

I began investigating your disappearance, I noted several other disappearances that you had been covering over the years. Entire periods of your life were just...blank. So I turned my investigation back to our home."

"You couldn't have found anything there. I...we left nothing behind."

"That is not true," Marcus said coldly. "You left me. All I had to do was put together the events of my childhood journal with the few records I could find about you. Then I compared them to local and international news stories. After I found your hidden bank deposits, the rest was easy."

"You don't understand," his father growled, sticking his finger in Marcus's face. "I crossed the wrong people and they found me. I took your mother and chartered a small plane. We crashed the plane to establish new identities!"

Marcus looked long and hard at his father. "But what about me?"

"The people following us never knew we had a son. You were safe."

"I am still safe," Marcus said.

"You just wouldn't let it go, would you? Others gave up their childhood fantasies...but you only studied harder. I checked up on your library account. You were reading some heavy material."

"Because I was serious about my goals. I still am."

"Your mother and I hoped that you would use your trust fund

money to become something respectable, Marcus. Something safe. Something…unlike the path we chose."

Marcus stood to his feet. For the first time, his father noticed that Marcus was two full inches taller than him.

"Once I discovered who you really were, I found out why you fled," Marcus said. "And that is when I hunted down the people you were running from."

Marcus produced a newspaper clip detailing a freak explosion at a Chinese mansion. "They had an accident."

His father stared at him wide-eyed. "You fool! You don't know who you're dealing with! They'll just send more people— they won't let this go!"

Marcus's father swung again, but this time, Marcus was prepared. He easily parried the blow and struck his father in the side of the head.

"Stop it!" Marcus said. "I don't care who you are. You will not hit me again. And I did use the money to better myself. That's what this was really about, isn't it? You were afraid that I would become a better spy than you. You were right to be afraid."

Marcus's father charged, but Marcus easily stepped to the side and turned, kicking his father in the head, sending him sprawling into the dirt. When his father tried to respond, Marcus landed blow after blow until his father did not get back up. Marcus heard a soft moan escape from his father's lips.

"I was hoping that this would have gone better," Marcus said, straightening his sleeves. "Don't worry about anyone else following you. I've already erased your identity in most international databases—something you failed to do. You are free to live your lives."

"How?" his father asked.

"You gave me life, so we are even," Marcus said, walking away. "I don't ever want to see either of you again. Tell mother I said goodbye."

Marcus's father lay bloody and dazed on the cold ground, watching his son walk away.

CHAPTER ONE

Ben Cole floored the tiny sedan, cursing himself for not renting something faster on his honeymoon. The only reason he had managed to keep up with the black sports car they were chasing was Nauru's narrow roads. He held the steering wheel tightly while Sarah, his new bride, contacted base. The smell of burnt oil escaped the tiny four-cylinder engine as Ben pushed it far past its manufacturer's limits. He knew that it was just a matter of time before the car burnt out from beneath him. Sarah entered the six-digit passcode and they heard the familiar beep over the car radio as they connected to their Mossad commander.

"Control, we have Eames in sight!" Sarah yelled over the radio. "We need backup!"

"Negative, Barracuda, you are not cleared to pursue."

"Control, I say again, Eames in sight!"

"Stand down, Barracuda."

Ben grimaced at the voice of his handler, smacking the steering wheel in frustration, but he took his foot off the accelerator and the sports car sped off into the distance, leaving only the throaty roar of its engine behind. Ben and Sarah would be just two more operatives on a long list of people who had tried—and failed—to capture Marcus Eames, one of the most elusive spies of the twentieth century. Ben knew that base had to have had a serious reason to order them to stand down. He just hoped it was a damn good one.

"Barracuda, comply!" the voice ordered.

"Complying," Sarah said and broke connection.

Ben watched the car speed off into the distance and his face echoed his frustration.

"Control told me to comply, not you," Sarah said with a sly smile.

"I knew there was a reason I loved you," Ben said, punching the accelerator.

Eames was only a few years older than Ben, but he was already a ghost—a legend among spies. He freely traded in secrets that normally would have resulted in death warrants, but after eight years of monumental failures trying to capture or kill him, no agency on Earth could risk pursuing him. Nations who sent operatives against him had their state secrets sold at auction to the highest bidders, while nations who turned a blind eye to his actions tended to survive unscathed. Eventually, most just tried to accommodate him, realizing that he was going to get the information that he wanted anyway.

Ben Cole and his new bride Sarah were more excited about investigating Marcus Eames than their honeymoon. They had been training together since they were teenagers, and, despite official policy, had fallen in love. This conflict of interest threatened to expel both from Mossad, Israel's famed intelligence agency, until Sarah noted that the agency needed sleeper cell couples. Why could they not really be a couple?

The answer was simple: the security of Israel could not be placed at risk because of a potential marital spat. Sarah pressed on, volunteering herself and Ben for psychological trials. Finally, after a battery of tests, an exception was granted and they were given an assignment in Egypt. While the Israeli government had recently signed a peace treaty with Egypt, there were several subversive elements threatening to topple the Egyptian government from within, introducing chaos into the Middle East.

There was already too much chaos in the Middle East.

After they were married, Ben and Sarah requested a "tropical honeymoon near Australia." Because Marcus Eames was considered a threat to the national security of Israel, Mossad gladly acquiesced to their request, sending them on a two-week tour of Nauru and Australia in order to glean whatever information they could on Marcus Eames. After finishing their honeymoon in Australia, they would become sleeper cells in Egypt for the next ten years.

This would be Ben's last chance at fieldwork for a decade.

Ben stomped the accelerator, but the sleek black sports car was no longer in sight.

If he could not outrace Eames, he would outthink him. There were only two ways off the island, boat or plane, and Ben could not imagine Eames increasing his exposure by waiting for a public boat. Now that he knew he was being pursued, Marcus would have to leave the island quickly.

That meant a private jet or private boat. Ben was counting on a jet—a boat would simply be too easy to catch, and Marcus would not risk capture.

Ben turned the car around, counter to everything he had been taught while tailing a suspect.

"What are you doing?" Sarah asked.

"Taking a gamble," Ben said.

Nauru's only airport was behind them. If Ben was right, and Marcus was going to fly out of Nauru, they might even be able to beat him to the airport. If he escaped, they would finish their stay in Nauru, gather what information they could, file a report and begin their mission in Egypt.

Ben's car screeched into the tiny airport. There was only one tarmac, and a plane sat near the hangar, ready to leave. Ben turned toward the plane to block its departure.

That was when the black sports car rammed the passenger side of his rental, rolling them twice.

To Ben, the world seemed to move in slow motion. The blocky shards of glass from the passenger door window flew around the interior like tiny diamonds. The combined sounds of groaning metal and smashing glass combined into an ethereal orchestra, and Ben could only hold on to the steering wheel with a sense of helplessness. He looked over at Sarah. Her long black hair was splayed in all directions as the car roof over her crumpled.

When everything settled, Ben was dazed and in pain. He did not know where he was.

He saw a thin man with light Polynesian skin walk toward the plane with a briefcase. Ben watched the plane leave and then he turned to see Sarah collapsed in the seat beside him.

Then everything went dark.

* * *

Ben sat up in his bed, trying to sort his dream from reality. The darkness of his room coincided with the last moment of the dream, so he instinctively reached over to Sarah.

But Sarah had been dead for a long time.

She had survived the wreck with nothing more than a small knot on her brow. Ben often joked that it proved just how hard her head was. The pair never got to finish their honeymoon. As soon as they were out of the hospital, they were sent to their mission in Egypt. Life was happy for the next few years. They established a small business and made friends. Things were good. They even considered remaining in Egypt after their mission was over.

Then a local governor kidnapped Sarah and raped her over a three-day period. When Ben took the case to court, the judge found Sarah guilty of adultery and she was stoned to death. The case against the governor was thrown out on a technicality.

Ben broke his cover, killing both the judge and the governor. None of his Mossad allies would help him. The governor had been too large a target. An American agent named Mark Cole gave his life helping Ben flee to America. Without his wife or his home country, Benjamin Maugaine was no more. He adopted his rescuer's last name as well as his country.

Benjamin Cole became a deadly commodity when it came to dealing with terrorists.

Over the course of his life, he had two recurring nightmares and losing Marcus Eames was one of them. The other was the day his wife was lead out of the courtroom to be stoned. The nightmares seemed to serve no purpose other than to remind him of his largest failures. He glanced at his alarm clock.

5:24 AM.

Six minutes before his alarm was set to go off.

Ben surrendered his remaining sleep to take his mind away from the unregulated lands of his subconscious. He made his bed the same way he had since his earliest days in the military, tight and flat. He showered quickly and brushed his teeth in the small but functional bathroom. After being given his current job, one of the many Presidential bunkers scattered across the country was taken off-grid and converted into his office. The St. Louis bunker was chosen due to its proximity to the nation's central internet hub, as well as its fort-like security. It was buried twelve stories beneath a bar whose only job was to protect the entrance.

Every scrap of processed information in North America passed through the computers behind the first door on the right. The technicians who were upgrading the hub assumed that it would only be accessible by the President, so Ben's system had access to everything the President's did. They also assumed that the other lines either went to Langley or the White House. They were not wrong. They did. They just happened to pass through a small sanitarium on the East Coast first, where a gray-faced man named Smith, Ben Cole's boss, worked.

Ben always chose to sleep in the bunker next to the main office room. The bunker was designed to house the eight-member core of the President's security staff. Ben never slept in the more luxurious Presidential quarters next door. He was not the President.

When he left his barracks, he entered an exact duplicate of the Oval Office. It boasted the familiar three-window diorama behind a classic wooden desk and circular Presidential rug. The only thing missing was the President.

Ben took his seat behind the desk and started the small coffee maker behind him. A hidden button beneath the front of the desk activated the office computers. The huge monitors that lined the walls began displaying information. The central monitor on the wall before him showed different angles of the bar above, alternating between infrared shots of the interior and parking lot. As it finally booted, the thin monitor on his desk displayed a copy of the Preamble to the Constitution and as always, Ben read the preamble to himself before logging on to proceed.

It was his daily prayer.

Ben added two teaspoons of caramel-flavored creamer to his coffee and began mindlessly stirring as the monitors began filling with seemingly random information. Message after message scrawled across the monitors. Ben knew these were the stories that were being prepared for the President's Daily Threat Matrix. The information would be assembled into a smaller report within the hour, but Ben liked looking at the raw information before it became a list of polished bullet points. Sometimes analysts left out things or even allowed their personal bias to draw unnecessary attention to or away from something.

Ben quickly sifted through the volumes of information flashing in front of him. Large money laundering deals were noted in Syria and Monaco—nothing new there. A reporter was beheaded as a threat to America.

Ben clenched his jaw and clicked to the next story. It seemed that almost every morning, he was given a new inspiration for his job. Human nature almost ensured that he would never be out of work.

Ben took another sip of his coffee and continued reading his briefing. After verifying that nothing of immediate urgency required his attention, Ben opened the document sent to him by Smith, detailing the Sinanju rite of negotiations. It was far longer than his morning read.

After reading several pages, he shook his head. It was hard to imagine Stone and Freya, his two Sinanju-trained field agents, following the arcane negotiation rituals described, rituals that included bows, salutations, and even poems. He allowed himself a brief smile while imagining Stone, muscular and gruff, sitting cross-legged on the floor reciting poetry.

CHAPTER TWO

His name was Winston Smith, but those who knew him called him Stone. Throughout his life, he had been called by many other names. In boarding school, he was first known as 'Master Winston' by his teachers, as well as 'Little Orphan Winnie' and 'Shovelhead' by his peers. He graduated early from boarding school and entered the Navy's SEAL program. While in SEAL training, he won every grueling test they were given, earning him the name 'Winner.'

On his first combat mission, he was paired with a SEAL nicknamed Dozer. The man was on his second tour of duty and objected to having to babysit the rookie. He followed orders, but he did not speak a single word to Winner as he led them into a thick El Salvadoran jungle.

Winner and Dozer had been assigned to a four-man team ordered to extract local informants in the dark of night and escort them safely out of the country. Dozer and Winner went south, while the other team members went west.

Shortly after entering hostile territory, Dozer and Winner encountered enemy fire.

"Damn it, a trap," Dozer muttered. "We'll bypass the hill on the east and engage the enemy from behind."

Dozer and Winner ducked and slowly headed east, the small sounds they were making hidden by the sound of several AK-47s. Dozer tossed a stun grenade back toward their earlier position to confuse the enemy. When the enemy saw the small flash, the gunfire stopped.

Dozer tugged on Winner to move more quickly. He heard Dozer mutter the word 'noob' before they saw the enemy. There were five rebel fighters, one of them looking toward their old position with night vision binoculars. The other four were sitting with their rifles relaxed, waiting for their leader's next order.

Dozer took aim and opened up with his custom M4. Three men jerked with each impact, falling lifelessly to the ground. The other two sprinted off into the darkness of the forest before being hit.

"Secure the area!" Dozer barked. "I'm going after them!"

It was the equivalent of giving him trash duty, but Winner followed orders to secure the area, grabbing the weapons from the downed men and standing behind them in a crouching position.

Suddenly he heard pistol fire from the forest.

Winner waited until the gunfire died down. The last rounds he heard were from the pistol.

"Dozer, is the area secure?" Winner asked softly over his radio. "Dozer?"

A soft crunch of branches to his left.

Winner wheeled around just in time to see the last rebel aiming his pistol at Winner and pulling his trigger. Time seemed to freeze for Winner. The man was too close to miss a headshot and he knew it. The empty click from his pistol vanquished the grin from the man's face. Winner returned the favor, showing him that his gun still had plenty of ammo.

The man's body seemed to dance to the beat of Winner's rifle and when he finally fell, the look of shock was still frozen on his face. Winner grabbed his pistol and headed toward the location of the gunfire. Winner could not imagine that the remaining rebel could have taken Dozer out with just a pistol, not with Dozer's years of experience and body armor. Winner ran around the west area to return to their original position when he saw the leaves dropping off in one area. He caught himself just before he would have fallen over a thirty-foot drop.

This was not on their topographical map.

Winner checked behind him one last time, but detected no movement. He went around the side of the cliff, slowly scaling down the rocky terrain. Winner found Dozer lying unconscious near the bottom of the small ravine behind some bushes. By the look at his vest, Dozer had been shot several times. His body armor had caught most of the bullets, but a slow trickling of blood had begun to pool beneath his left thigh. One of the bullets had struck an artery and Dozer was bleeding out.

Winner dropped his backpack and secured a tourniquet around

Dozer's upper thigh. A quick examination of the leg allowed Winner to feel the bullet still inside the meat of his leg.

If Winner had done everything right, Dozer would live. His problem was getting a two-hundred-pound man back to the landing zone. It was six miles back in wild terrain and the pick-up was scheduled in a little over two hours.

Winner's radio came alive with the sound of static and gunfire.

"Dozer, this is Moon Knight. Target acquired. We are under fire. Return to base immediately!"

"Roger, Moon Knight. This is Winner. Dozer is down. Returning to base."

There was no reply.

Winner rolled Dozer on top of his sleeping bag and strapped both their rifles around his shoulder. He grabbed the end of the sleeping bag and dragged Dozer to the landing zone. He only stopped for occasional drinks of water to offset the heat of the jungle that seemed to suck the fluids from his body. Winner ignored the heat, ignored the increasing pain in his legs and feet, concentrating on his steps, one after another. When he finally reached the target area, Winner collapsed. Both he and Dozer were returned to the states and placed in medical care.

Both men recovered, but Winner was told that during the rescue he had sustained damage to his left heel. Winner was relieved that it wasn't more serious, until he was told that it was severe enough to give him a one-way ticket out of the Navy. Two weeks later, Winner was packing to leave base for what he knew was the last time, when he found a small note under his socks. Dozer wanted to meet him off base at a local coffee house.

Winner finished packing and arrived at the coffee house an hour later. Dozer was already seated toward the back where it was darker. He motioned for Winner to sit beside him. Though he was still recovering from his wounds, only an arm sling was visible. Winner could imagine how many drugs were pumping through his system.

"Why all the secrecy?" Winner asked as he sat down. "I'm already out of the loop."

"I always pay back my debts," Dozer said. "How's the heel?"

"That's funny you ask. You're busted up and almost die and they let you stay, but Uncle Sam takes one look at my heel and doesn't want to take a chance of it failing in a mission," Winner explained. "On the plus side, I now have this shiny VA card and two years of separation pay."

"I never heard of someone injuring their heel, man," Dozer said, shaking his head. "But you injured it by dragging my fat ass six miles, so I owe you. Here," Dozer said, handing Winner a small piece of paper. "If you want to keep doing what we do and make a good living at the same time, just give this guy a call."

"What's this?"

"Small time merc operations. You know, bag and grab stuff.

Everything is off the radar, but it's all sanctioned by the spooks, so unlike most mercs, we're only playing on our side," Dozer said. "It's what I'll be doing after my stint ends in October."

"I thought you would re-up?" Stone asked.

"Nope, I got what I came here for," Dozer said, pointing at the small piece of paper in Winner's hand. "Contacts like these are worth gold. I paid my dues. Now it's time to rake in the cash. You'll see what I mean. You'll be able to retire in three years."

Winner took the number and made the call. For the next few months, he found all the mercenary work he wanted. He performed relatively safe operations throughout Central America, and, just as Dozer said, he was making more for one job than he had for his entire duration in the SEAL team. The only thing that irritated him was the way the local people pronounced his name. It sounded like they were calling him 'Weiner.' He decided to change his name to something stronger. He tried going back to "Winston" for all of one day, but they pronounced it "Ween-stone."

From that day forward, he just went by Stone.

Stone went to base to get his next set of orders when his contact gave him a warning. A report said that Dozer had killed his commanding officer and was *persona non grata.*

"You want to stay in the network, you stay away from Dozer," his contact said.

"What happened?" Stone asked.

"The official story or what really happened?"

"Duh," Stone replied.

"A month before Dozer checks out, his unit gets called to Afghanistan. It's a two-year tour. He shows up drunk during commander's call, said a few things about the commanding officer's mother. That got everyone's attention. The CO busted him to E-nothing, and gave him his walking papers while his unit was deployed. Then some idiot murdered the commanding officer."

"Dozer?"

"Nah, he was on his way out," his contact said. "Just bad timing."

"If he's innocent, why is he blackballed?"

"We don't need heat, kid," the contact said.

"Dozer got me this job," Stone mused.

"You still had better stay away from him. Will that be a problem?"

"No, sir," Stone said and the subject never came up again.

On Stone's next mission, he met his father. No matter how he had imagined meeting him as an orphan, he could never have dreamed it would be this way. At first, Remo Williams seemed like any other person, but the things he could do were almost magical. That was because his father was a Master of Sinanju, the greatest of all martial arts. Long before kung fu, before karate, before ninjit-su, there was Sinanju. Every martial art was based off a tiny beam of light from the sun that was Sinanju. The small Korean village of Sinanju had been the source of the greatest assassins in the world throughout its five-thousand-year history, and the skills of the Masters of Sinanju were the stuff of legend.

Masters of Sinanju did not just break boards with their hands—they could liquefy steel and turn solid rock into dust. Masters of Sinanju did not use their fists as meat mallets to strike like other martial arts; they were delicate enough to manipulate an enemy's nerves to take control of their bodies.

So when his father told Stone that he had a grandfather named Sunny Joe, who was the chief of a tribe in Arizona, Stone decided to take some time off and find out about his roots.

Stone quickly learned that the tribe in Arizona was an offshoot of the House of Sinanju in Korea. Many centuries earlier, a blind Master had inadvertently trained both his twin sons in the art of Sinanju. Because it was forbidden to train more than one pupil, Kojong, one of the twin boys, left his homeland and set sail across the Great Sea, settling in what was eventually to be known as America.

The reservation was where Stone first met his half-sister, Freya. She was born from a different mother and was much younger than he was, but Stone quickly found out that she was no pushover. She had been raised a half-world away and had been breathing properly for her entire life, and took to their grandfather's Sinanju training much easier than Stone. Breathing and diet were the first keys to fully unlocking Sinanju, but Stone was still trying to quit smoking, and he was still known for his love of meat and pastries.

Stone's training was more grueling than anything he had encountered in the military, but he soon was able to do things that earlier he would have believed to be impossible. He began learning how to dodge a bullet and score metal with his fingernails. Yet, despite his skill, Stone knew that he was just starting out on the path of Sinanju.

He and Freya had volunteered to work for a secret organization, helping to secure America's borders to serve as a lethal response team to terrorist sleeper cells. Though their missions had been successful, Stone realized that luck had been just as much of a factor as their Sinanju abilities, and both Stone and Freya realized that they needed more training.

That is what worried him.

Freya was further advanced in her Sinanju training, and had recently undergone something she called "The Night of Salt," where her body permanently changed to better adapt to Sinanju. She had become inhumanly strong and fast, but her digestive system had changed to process every molecule of every nutrient in her food. She was now restricted to a meager diet consisting almost entirely of rice and fish. Eating a hamburger or pizza would put her in a coma—or worse.

Seeing how much Freya's life had changed from her Sinanju

training made Stone question whether or not he wished to stay on the path. Once you went far enough in Sinanju, there was no turning back.

* * *

Stone walked to their training hut and noticed that the south wall had still not been repaired. Freya had accidentally damaged it and Sunny Joe told her to fix it. She was normally strong enough to do such work herself. In fact, she normally could have done the job better than Stone, but she had recently broken her ribs by saving them both from an explosion. When she came to ask for his help rebuilding the south wall of the hut, she had not purposely given him sad puppy-dog eyes—at least Stone did not think she had—but there was no way he could refuse his kid sister.

"Doesn't grandpa own a hammer?" Stone asked as he dug through the pile of wood. "I thought he was kidding when he told you to hammer the nails in with your finger."

The young blonde haired girl sitting on top of the large boulder at the front of the hut smiled.

"Grandfather wanted me to drive the nails in with my fingertips as an exercise in focus," she said. "Would you like to try it?"

"No thanks," Stone said. "I'm not ready for that stuff yet."

Stone continued looking around the back of the damaged hut. But though he found a large sack of nails, there was no hammer in sight. He closed his eyes in frustration. "Okay, fine. What do I do?"

"It's not hard, really," Freya said cheerfully, trying to reassure him. "It just takes focus. Center yourself and then see yourself pushing your finger through the board. Not too hard though or the nail will bend."

"Just like that, huh?" Stone asked. He set one of the boards against the wall and held a nail in front of it.

"Breathe deeply," Freya said, trying to mimic a deep breath. A sharp and ragged coughing session told both her and Stone that she was not able to breathe properly, much less center herself. For someone whose body had remained perfectly centered the majority of her life, Stone knew that had to be incredibly frustrating.

"Stop," Stone said. "I'll do it."

Freya tried to hold in a cough, but failed. As soon as she finished coughing, she concentrated on the nail with Stone, as if their combined mental might would help the nail to go through more easily.

Stone drew in a deep breath to center his body, and the world around him seemed to slow to a halt. As his senses expanded, he was able to detect a small spider moving at the edge of the windowsill. His mind mapped each dust particle as they danced lazily around him. Then he turned his attention to the nail he held with his left hand.

Stone turned his focus inward until the nail was all he could see. Stone could sense the strength of the steel that the nail was constructed of just as surely as if he had chemically measured it. Then he drew his fist back, holding out his index finger as if he were going to poke it.

Stone struck.

He felt the soft tissue at the end of his fingertip make contact with the nail, followed quickly by the bone behind it. The small bursa sacs between each joint compressed, but it was not until Stone felt the pressure reach his knuckle that he realized that he had struck with too much speed and too little force.

His finger ricocheted off the nail and Stone brought his hand to his chest. He jumped around the hut, flinging curses around like confetti.

Freya jumped off the boulder and started to reach for him.

"Are you okay?"

"No!" Stone yelled. "I just jammed my finger back into my frickin' wrist!"

Freya took one look at the dark bruise already forming and ran from the hut.

"I will find a hammer!" she yelled back.

CHAPTER THREE

Anyone driving west on Arizona's Guadalupe Canyon Road would only notice the Sinanju tribe by the small sign two miles outside of the reservation's borders. If they did not miss the narrow dirt road leading to the reservation, the next thing they would see would be a large red sign reading *MOTEL SINANJU.* The long, one-story building under the sign was constructed three decades earlier by the Arizona state tourism board. They had built several cheap motels to attract tourism dollars to various areas of the state, but, like the others, the Motel Sinanju failed to bring in any tourists, and the government eventually abandoned the project. The only proof that the building was not abandoned was the dimly-blinking VACANCY sign on the front.

Most of the people who stopped at the reservation were looking for cheap tobacco or a casino, neither of which existed on the Sinanju reservation. When the state decided to stop funding the motel, the Sinanju tribe offered to take up maintenance in exchange for ownership and reduced electricity rates.

The motel quickly turned into an unofficial tribal storage facility. The man who operated the motel had little to do, but he received free rent and board. Two of the twenty rooms were kept open for any travelers who wandered into the area.

Over the past thirty-two years, the Motel Sinanju had rented out the rooms twenty-eight times. For several members of the tribe, that was twenty-eight times too many. The Sinanju tribe prided themselves on their isolation from the outside world.

So when a hungry nineteen-year-old boy named Tekoa showed up at the council headquarters, people began talking. Some said he was just a hippie looking for an experience. Others feared that he was a descendant of the original tribal leaders who had been banned from the reservation centuries earlier. Despite the vocal objection of a few villagers, however, the council gave him temporary lease for a year at one of the motel rooms, citing an old tribal law that protected expatriates from other tribes. The council did this without notifying Bill Roam, the chief, so when Bill called for a meeting with Tekoa, the young man was nervous.

Tekoa did not have to ask where Bill Roam's office was. Everyone knew. It was a small building sandwiched next to the council chambers. He took one look at the door, took a deep breath, and walked in.

As soon as he entered, he was greeted by the smell of old magazines. Two steps in, he walked onto a floorboard that creaked so loudly that he thought his foot was going to fall through. An elderly man was sitting behind the counter, grinning at his misfortune.

"Everyone thinks that board is gonna break," Dale said. "But even though it's old, it's desert ironwood."

"You're...Dale, right?" Tekoa asked, timidly.

"Unless I'm late coming home," Dale replied, offering a

handshake. "Dale Barker. I'm the historian-slash-grunt around here."

"Tommy told me that chief Bill wants to see me," he said, accepting the handshake.

"Never call him Bill, son. We call our chief 'Sunny Joe.' He's in his office."

"The council said I could stay a year," Tekoa said, worried. "I still have a few months left."

"Though he rarely does it, Sunny Joe has the power to veto the council's decision, so don't rile him," Dale said. "Have a seat. I'll let him know you're here."

Tekoa sat on the cracked leather sofa against the wall of the small office. He grabbed one of the magazines from the end table. Though it looked unread, it was dated March 1981.

Dale returned to the counter and lowered his head for a violent series of coughs.

"Sunny Joe said he'll be with you in a minute," he said. "You need something to drink?"

"Nah," Tekoa said. "Am I in trouble?"

"If you were in trouble with Sunny Joe, you wouldn't still be here," Dale said. "He just has a few questions."

Tekoa noticed as a tall, thin man appeared behind the counter. It was eerie. His feet made no sound as he walked across the dry wooden floor. And while Sunny Joe looked to be in his fifties, Tekoa knew he was much older.

"This way," Sunny Joe said, but Tekoa could not tell if he was angry.

Sunny Joe sat behind a modest desk, which was far more organized than Tekoa would have assumed from the chaos of paperwork in the front office. He motioned for Tekoa to sit in one of the two chairs in front of his desk. Unlike the worn sofa out front, these chairs, like the rest of Sunny Joe's office, had been well taken care of.

"Let's start at the beginning," Sunny Joe said. "Where did you say you came from?"

"The Coushatta in Texas," Tekoa said.

"I know the chief down there. Nice guy. So what brings you to Arizona?" Sunny Joe asked.

Tekoa bent over just a bit before answering.

"I need a new home," he said quietly.

"Your home is with the Coushatta," Sunny Joe said. "The Sinanju are a closed tribe."

"I was sent away from my tribe and my grandmother suggested that I might find a home here," Tekoa said, taking a breath before continuing. "I'm...cursed."

"Cursed?" Sunny Joe asked. "What do you mean?"

Tekoa sat back and then averted his eyes to the floor as if embarrassed.

"It started out bad. I'm an only child, and I was born under a bad sign. My parents always tried to protect me, but last year, our home burnt down. When they moved the rubble, both of my parents were dead. I was lying near them, but the fire and the smoke didn't harm me. The chief said that I died, but my soul was not finished. I was a 'walking spirit,' he said, and no longer a part of the tribe. My grandmother gave me enough money to take a train."

"But why come here?" Sunny Joe asked. "The Coushatta are all the way on the other side of Texas."

"My grandmother told me of this place. 'The Sinanju are magical warriors,' she said. You must try to live there."

"Your grandmother has no right to send you here."

"I know that," Tekoa said humbly. "But I have never lived off a reservation and I have nowhere to go."

Sunny Joe looked at the boy. He was lying about something, but his anguish was real.

"Against my advice, the council gave you a year to find another place," Sunny Joe said. "Have you found work yet? If you don't work, you don't eat."

"I've been helping out as everyone needs me."

"What happened at the basketball court?"

"Tommy and Matt were yelling at Freya. I tried to keep the situation calm, but Tommy went too far. Called Freya a man and told her that she didn't belong here."

"That all?"

"Uh, Freya grabbed the basketball goal by the pole and smashed it to the ground," Tekoa said, still not believing what he had seen.

"And you had nothing to do with that?" Sunny Joe asked suspiciously.

"No, absolutely not!" Tekoa said defensively. "I'm just trying to make my peace here. In fact, I'd like to become a member of your tribe."

"Do you even know what Sinanju is?"

"Your tribal martial art. Some in the Coushatta say that the power of the old gods is in your blood. I have never seen anyone do what Freya did. I'd say Sinanju is pretty powerful, whatever it is."

"You should also know that it allows me to realize when someone is lying about something. You haven't told the truth since you got here. My pop would've just squeezed you until you told the truth, but I'm going to do something worse: I'm going to hold off my recommendation for you to stay here until you tell me what you're lying about."

"But...I'm not lying," Tekoa said, though his eyes were not as confident as his voice.

Sunny Joe easily detected the slight pause in his breath, the quick jerk his eyes made to the left when he spoke. The increased heart rate and slight flush to his face.

"Well, you're not very good at lying, so you have that in your defense. Like I told you, I give you until the end of the year. After that, you're gone," Sunny Joe said in a manner that Tekoa knew that it was time for him to leave.

Tekoa started to say something but then just said, "Thank you, Mr. Sunny Joe."

As he left, Dale came in and sat down in front of Sunny Joe's desk. He looked tired, but Sunny Joe knew that look in his eye.

"Don't start on me, Dale," Sunny Joe cautioned.

"Ain't often we get youngsters wanting to come *to* the

reservation," Dale said. "Sunny Joe, we can't afford to turn people away!"

"I understand, but..."

"There's no buts, Bill!" Dale interrupted. "We're a dying tribe! Unless you find a way to make babies out of sand, we aren't going to exist in the next hundred years!"

Sunny Joe was not used to his friend interrupting him, but pain had caused Dale to be more agitated lately.

"Careful, Dale. You're starting to sound like Paul," Sunny Joe said, referring to the head of the Sinanju tribal council.

Ever since he became the head of the tribal council, Paul Moore had never agreed with Sunny Joe's decisions. Whether the topic was federal rights or funding, Sunny Joe could always count on a fight from Paul Moore.

"Then this would be the only time," Dale said. "I'm nothing like Paul."

Dale knew why Paul and Sunny Joe did not get along, although he could never tell Sunny Joe. After Sunny Joe's mother had died, his father Joseph Roam had begun a relationship with Paul's mother. When she became pregnant with Paul, Joseph moved her to the outskirts of the reservation to avoid the stigma of producing a bastard child. No one would ever know who the father was.

But the Sinanju people were not a merciful people.

The taunts were merciless and constant, and soon the widow refused to set foot outside her home. She tried keeping her son Paul out of school, but Joseph insisted that he go. When it became too much, she demanded that she and Paul be allowed to leave the tribe.

Joseph tried to quietly pull money from the tribal coffers to take care of her, but the council got wind of what he was doing, though not why. They held a secret meeting to remove Joseph from office. Dale was present as tribal historian, but he would rather not have been there at all. He knew that Joseph Roam was not a patient man and not used to explaining his actions to others. He showed up at the meeting and all but gave the tribal leader a stroke. Then he demanded a recount.

The council voted unanimously to authorize the funds and restated their public support to Joseph's tribal authority.

It was around this time that Bill's wife had died in childbirth and he had left the tribe. He had ended up in Hollywood performing as a stunt man. Joseph had to make a decision: would he train Paul in Sinanju, or would he wait for Bill to return?

The answer was easy. Paul had just graduated high school, far too old to begin training in the Sun Source. So from time to time, Joseph would make trips to California to visit Bill, trying to convince him to return home.

Dale never told Sunny Joe about his half brother, and he knew better than to list it in the records.

"Let me tell you about Paul Moore," Sunny Joe said. "He went out of his way this morning to tell me that the council was considering granting the boy Sinanju status over any of my objections."

"Stop making me agree with him," Dale said. "We need new

blood, Sunny Joe."

"He better be glad that he's dealing with me and not my pop. Doesn't it raise red flags to any of you that the boy is lying about something important?"

"Kids lie sometimes," Dale said. "Maybe it's something small."

"Dale, this isn't about breaking curfew or cheating in school. His body language is trying to hide something big. He won't get my vote of support until I know what he's lying about."

Dale leaned back and took a breath and began coughing. "Sorry," he managed to say. "I shouldn't have yelled."

"You have a lot on your plate these days, Dale," Sunny Joe said, putting his hand on his friend's shoulder. "What did Doc Hodges say?"

Dale looked down in embarrassment. "He said that I might want to try something from the old ways."

"He didn't even try to recommend any modern medicine?"

"Pain medicine he gave me hasn't been doing the job, Sunny Joe. I gotta double the dosage just to feel it now."

"That's not very smart. Didn't he give you any alternatives?"

"You know Doc Hodges, Sunny Joe. If he gets half a chance to recommend turtle paste, he's gonna prescribe it."

"Which would be funny if your life weren't on the line."

"He gave me a list," Dale said, pulling a folded piece of paper from his pocket.

"This isn't turtle paste," Sunny Joe said, reading the list. "This is his daddy's old tea remedy. He's just mixing chamomile tea with honey and adding kimchi leaves and garlic. Nothing there that can hurt you, but I also don't see anything there that would heal you, either."

Dale lowered his head. He paused before he looked back at Sunny Joe.

"You were telling Freya that breathing exercises will help her heal," Dale almost whispered. "Do you think it would work for me?"

Sunny Joe knew his friend's immense desperation for even asking such a question. As chief historian for the tribe, Dale knew better than to ask for Sinanju training, regardless of the reason.

"You know that I'm supposed to kick your butt off the reservation for even asking something like that," Sunny Joe said sternly. "Don't do that to me, Dale."

Dale bent over the desk and took a deep breath and tried to suppress a cough. He looked defeated. "I had to ask, Sunny Joe. I have nothing else but Doc Hodges' magical tea."

"I wouldn't call any tea that had kimchi and garlic 'magical,'" Sunny Joe said. "But let me see what I can do."

"Just give the boy a chance, Sunny Joe," Dale said. "He's been a pretty good helper."

"If you get him to admit what he is lying about, Dale, then I'll talk to him again."

CHAPTER FOUR

Marcus Eames had returned to Nauru for only the fourth time since his parents' disappearance. The last time he was here, a special session of the Nauruan parliament had given him Nauru's highest medal and appointed him to a special lifelong position as Nauru's 'Foreign Liaison.' His official job was to travel to various countries as he saw fit, looking out for Nauru. The parliament knew of his unofficial 'information-collecting activities,' but had turned a blind eye—Nauru had greatly profited from Marcus's reputation as the world's most powerful spy.

For Marcus to be summoned back to Nauru meant that something was seriously wrong, but Marcus did not put on a disguise or sneak into the parliament building. He pulled his car into the Chief Justice's parking spot.

As a small island nation of only nine thousand people, the Nauruan parliament building looked more like an upscale beach house than the meeting place of a nation's officials. Marcus exited the car and appeared to take a glance at his cell phone, but he was really surveying the grounds using the observational methods he had mastered from the monk's book.

Front of building suffering from the same mold present the last time I was here.

Eight cars parked in front. One is a visitor. Running plates before entering building.

President owns same car. New tires.

Three groundskeepers at work on the west side of the building.

National flag at three-quarters mast. Possible signal.

Marcus ran the plates on the only car he did not recognize. The car belonged to the treasurer's daughter. Marcus made a small note on his cell phone and entered through the front door, ignoring the stunned look on the face of the president's secretary. Marcus did not stop to ask where the president was. It was his job to know such things.

Marcus swung both doors of the president's office open with a flourish. The president's smile disappeared as he made eye contact with Marcus. They both knew why he was there. And though it had been years since the two men had last seen each other, Marcus had aged much better than the bloated and balding man who sat behind the presidential desk.

"I will call you back, dear," he said, hanging up the phone.

Opening his briefcase, Marcus placed several documents marked *TOP SECRET* on top of the president's tidy desk.

"You've been a very busy man," Marcus said.

The president instantly recognized most of the documents.

Marcus looked at the president of his country with disgust. The man, like the president before him, had no pride in their tiny country.

The president cleared his voice, though he could not maintain eye contact with Marcus.

"The United States is now dealing directly with terrorists. They pay ransoms quietly and resolve situations peacefully. You were so important that they sent the American Secretary of State last week to ask us for a personal favor."

"If that man is asking for a favor, then money is involved," Marcus said.

"To be honest, the United States wishes us to, uh…spare them from any of your future…ventures, at least until the end of the current administration," the president said quietly. "They have plans to invest in Nauru solar power for the next decade."

"Strings, Mr. President are always attached to foreign money," Marcus said with a steely glare that made the president feel like he had been caught stealing a cookie from the cookie jar. "How can you lead our nation when you are for sale?"

"I am responsible for the entire nation," the president stammered, trying to gain the moral high road. "And it is larger than you, Marcus!"

"It doesn't seem to be larger than your bank account," Marcus said and slid a printout of the president's personal bank records across the desk. A recent deposit for two million dollars was highlighted.

Marcus looked down his nose at the president as if the older man were a bug. "What did they tell you to do?"

The president grabbed a deep breath and, though he tried to show bravery, beads of sweat were already rolling down his brow.

"The decision has already been made, Mr. Eames. Effective two days ago, we terminated your post as Foreign Liaison," he said.

"Mr. Eames now, is it? Did you forget to tell me something else you did?" Marcus said. "As of yesterday at noon, you personally revoked my Nauruan citizenship. I am now a man without a country."

The president pulled out a small briefcase from beneath the desk and slid it toward Marcus. "The United States has arranged to have you exiled. They promise your safety as long as you remain quiet. They have even set up a small Argentinian safe house for you."

"And you believed them," Marcus noted, almost shaking his head. The man was so naïve.

"Marcus, please, don't make this harder than it has to be," the president said. "Let me...aid in your transition," the president said, hand sliding towards his checkbook.

"I do not need your money."

"Marcus, you've stirred too many hornets' nests. You had to know this day was coming!"

"Perhaps, but I thought that if it did, it would come because my president made a decision based on what was right for Nauru—not because some overseas bureaucrat ordered him to do so while writing him a check."

The window to the left of the president's office shattered as two gas canisters crashed through. Marcus grabbed a deep breath and leapt behind the desk. He punched the president in the stomach, ensuring that he would grab a deep lungful of whatever they were pumping into the office. Marcus inserted a pair of nose filters from his jacket pocket and pulled out his gloves. He had seen the men posing as gardeners when he entered. Nauru did not have a budget for three groundskeepers.

Besides, the men were working far too hard to be government employees.

Marcus was surprised about one thing: he did not think they would actually attempt a capture while the president was present.

The president was obviously naïve enough to assume that the US forces would be able to take Marcus without much of a fight. He was wrong.

Marcus was already positioned beside the window when the first soldier enetered. Expecting to find two unconscious men on the floor, the man was surprised by a quick karate chop to the throat. That distracted him long enough for Marcus to fire his gun directly into the man's face.

Another explosion of glass came from the other side window and two more men entered, firing as they cleared the window frame. A bullet scraped Marcus's side as he dodged toward the president's desk, but his bulletproof jacket dulled the impact. Overturning the desk and using it as a makeshift shield, Marcus grabbed his briefcase and knocked the president to the floor.

"I should leave you sitting up," Marcus spat, but knew that to do so while men were shooting would be a death sentence for the president. Marcus knew that if the president were shot, the blame would fall on him, so he pulled the unconscious man behind the overturned desk.

Bullets filled the air above him and Marcus whispered a soft prayer of thanks that the president before this one had chosen a quality desk. Marcus unlatched the briefcase and tossed it toward the two agents. As the hinge snapped open, a contact grenade exploded from within, catching both men partially in its blast. The men tried to gain their bearings, but Marcus was around the desk before they could recover. He slid his knife between the slits in their body armor and kicked the rifles from their hands. He crushed their throats with his heel when they hit the floor and held them still until they no longer squirmed. His eyes remained glued to the window, looking for further interference.

After a minute, satisfied that the attack was over, Marcus took one last look at the president of his nation, unconscious on the floor behind his desk. Tears came to Marcus's eyes. It was not because of the incapacitating gas, but because his nation had betrayed him. They had not betrayed him because they felt that Marcus had done something wrong. Instead, he had been betrayed for money.

It was time to remind the world who the people of Nauru were. They were no longer the tiny guano-peddling nation of the past. Marcus had mostly stayed away from United States operations in the past because he could tell that they intended to do well, even if their actions were often misguided. But now they had placed themselves between him and his homeland.

It was time for Marcus Eames to remind them that all power comes at a cost.

CHAPTER FIVE

Stone and Freya moved their training mats toward the front of the still-damaged hut to avoid the dirt clods and wood planks stacked at the back. Sunny Joe stood to the side of the Founder's Stone, away from the entrance. Freya's face, normally a sponge for information, looked sad. Sunny Joe immediately recognized the look of boredom on Stone's face.

Sunny Joe smiled.

"For the record, I hated negotiations training, too," he said. "Yet it is as vital as breathing to a Master of Sinanju. While we are never to compete against the Korean House, we are still obligated to train in case the House ever needs our services."

"Okay, then I have a serious question," Stone said. "If we're getting paid to kill, how is this *not* competing against the Korean house again?"

"You and your sister are hiring yourselves out to the current employer of the House, America. If you hired out to any other country, you would be in competition. And then, if your dad found out, you would most likely be dead."

"So if Remo…" Stone said.

"Your dad," Sunny Joe corrected.

"Fine. If our *dad* were hired out to some maniac, we would have to work for them as well?"

"I didn't write the rules, son, but we're going to abide by them. You don't have to hire yourself out to anyone if you don't like the ruler. Sinanju is not slavery."

"But if our father is already working for America, don't we fall under him?" Freya asked.

"Nope. Your dad's contracts only cover him. That's why Master Chiun asked to see your contract when he saw you at your birthday."

"I wondered why he shook his head like that when I told him we didn't have a contract," Stone said. "What did he mean when he said that the 'babies would go to the sea'?"

"In the old days, when famine came to the Korean House, there wasn't enough food to go around. We had to send our babies home to the sea."

"They were drowned?" Stone asked, shocked. "That's awful!"

"Is it? It's easy to say that while sitting comfortably in our nice homes with refrigerators full of food, running water and air conditioning. We don't have to hunt. We just go down the block and buy food at the general store. In the old days, if you didn't have enough food, saving a baby that couldn't hunt or fish was the same as condemning it to death."

"I saw much poverty when my mother took me around Europe. There were days when we had nothing to eat until mother killed something," Freya said. "But it is still hard to imagine a poverty so great you would sacrifice your own children."

"Would you rather sit and watch them slowly starve to death?"

Freya lowered her head and remained silent as she tried to keep the scenario from playing in her mind.

"If you pay close enough attention during negotiations, your descendants will never have to experience it."

"Still sounds like a shakedown to me," Stone said.

"We are asked for our services. They are prepared for negotiation ceremonies and consider it to be the most dreaded aspect of a Sinanju contract. It is up to our clients to decide whether or not to hire us, but make no mistake: negotiation is a form of attack, and we have many weapons in our negotiations arsenal. If I had known that you were going to need these skills so soon, we would have covered them earlier, but we don't have time, so I'll just skip the historical accounts."

"Wow, you must really be pressed for time if we're gonna skip the scrolls," Stone said sarcastically. "How can we possibly understand the vast significance behind our actions if we don't hear about what Master Dingaling did thousands of years ago?"

"Don't worry," Sunny Joe said, smiling at Stone. "When you get back, I'll be sure to catch you up."

"Looking forward to it," Stone said, wishing he had kept his mouth shut.

Sunny Joe took a deep breath and closed his eyes. "Stone, you will need to center for this."

"For negotiations? Really? Am I going to have to dodge a ball point pen or something?"

Sunny Joe glared. "You've gotta last longer than your client. Center."

Stone grabbed a breath and forced it deep into the bottom of his lungs. He felt the refreshing wave of power washing over him, temporarily subduing the desire for nicotine. Freya sat quietly beside him, embarrassed. She was normally in a constantly-centered state, but while her ribs were still injured, it hurt her too much to breathe properly. Sunny Joe noticed the dejected look on her face.

"You've just gotta give your body time to heal, Freya," Sunny Joe said. "You're lucky to be alive."

"I'm just not used to feeling this…small," Freya finally said. "I feel unplugged from my own body."

"Keep up the exercises I gave you. Your body will heal soon enough."

"Yes, grandfather," Freya said with a sad acceptance. "How will this affect my negotiations?"

"Since you can't center, Stone will take lead on this one," Sunny Joe said.

"It all comes down to me? Can't she at least read the Ung poem?" Stone asked, referring to the unique style of Korean poetry that was measured in hours, not lines. Ung poetry was always considered vital to Sinanju negotiations—which Stone guessed was because most people would agree to anything in order to bring an end to the tedium.

Most Ung poems were the revelations of nature to a centered Master of Sinanju, who observed things as they slowly unfolded. The act of a bee landing on a flower took only a few seconds, but a Master of Sinanju saw many hundreds of things happening at once and the Ung poem would record each separate event. Such a poem would be considered an extremely brief Ung poem, measuring as little as two hours.

"Afraid not," Sunny Joe said. "One of the reasons for the Ung poem is to strain the endurance of your negotiator. Bottom line, when centered, we can remain perfectly still in one position for days. Our negotiators can't, so we start with an advantage."

"We still have to hear it," Stone moaned.

"Alright, let's get started," Sunny Joe said, ignoring Stone's protests. "What is the order of negotiations?"

Freya held her hand up.

"Sorry, but Stone needs to know this."

Stone frowned for a moment and then looked up in thought. "Give me a second. I know this. Formal greeting, then...wait, what am I supposed to call him? He's not a King or Pharaoh or anything."

"Hmmm, that's a good question," Sunny Joe said. "What do

you think, Freya?"

"You once said he is our chief of operations," Freya said thoughtfully. "How about Chieftain?"

"Do you really expect me to call him 'Chieftain Cole'?" Stone asked with a scoff.

"For the duration of the negotiations, yes," Sunny Joe said. "The first part of negotiations emphasize a person's power, so that later when you ask of them a simple thing such as sitting on the floor, or a larger amount of money, they will be too embarrassed to do otherwise."

"Chieftain Cole it is. Okay, formal greeting, thank the client for hiring Sinanju…uh," Stone stroked his chin.

Freya leaned forward, momentarily forgetting her troubles. "Presentation," she whispered.

"I got this!" Stone snapped. "Gimme a minute!"

"That's another thing," Sunny Joe said, interrupting. "On more than one occasion, I have heard how you treat each other in public. That stops right now. We are Sinanju. In private, you can fight like cats and dogs, but in public, you will treat each other as professionals."

"Yes, grandfather," Freya said.

"We already talked about that," Stone said. "I'm working on it."

"This is not an option, Stone. In public, your sister is to be treated as your equal," Sunny Joe said, sternly. "No exceptions!"

"Gotcha. Sorry, grandpa."

"If you're truly going to change, there is no need for an apology."

"Okay, formal greeting, thank the leader for choosing Sinanju, presentation of the first Ung poem...the bee and flower one, I think."

"Right, that is the shortest one," Sunny Joe said. "This is to let them mistakenly think that they can handle the longer ones afterward if they are needed."

"I still hate it. Okay, then confirm with client job specifics and pay, ask for our increases, minimum of...thirty percent?" Stone asked Sunny Joe.

"If you're a good negotiator, it will allow you room to be talked down to twenty-five percent. If you get talked down to ten percent you will be considered a failure. If you feel you are not getting what you want, start an Ung Poem of no less than four hours as a celebration of our proposed contract."

"Wow, which Ung poem will I choose?" Stone thought, thinking of the hundreds to choose from and trying not to groan audibly.

"Your choice," Sunny Joe said. "My favorite is the bear preparing for hibernation."

"Yeah, I have no favorite Ung poem," Stone said making a face to back up his statement. "Besides, I have another problem. The reason that Freya originally was going to read the Ung poems was because there is no way I can stay in a lotus position for four hours reading an Ung Poem. I can't stay centered for longer than an hour. Maybe ninety minutes if I push it."

"Then you'll just need to make sure these negotiations take less than two hours and end strongly in your favor," Sunny Joe said, winking.

"Do I gotta use a quill?" Stone asked.

"No. Only the final version has to be quill on parchment. After negotiations have been finalized, you will make two copies—one for the client and one for Dale. On site, Freya can do all of the writing with a normal pen," Sunny Joe said. "Legibly."

"I will do my best," Freya said. She had very good handwriting.

"How long should the contract be?" Stone asked. "I hope we don't have to do this every year."

"That's been a great debate among the Masters over the centuries," Sunny Joe said, proud that Stone actually thought it through. "A few insist on ten- or twenty-year contracts to ensure long-term income. Most insisted on contracts for specific duties or a limited number of years, because then you're able to negotiate higher rates each time. Since you are just starting out, a four-year contract for general services would be acceptable."

"We'll have to do this again in four years?" Stone asked with a numb look on his face.

"Believe me, if you do this correctly, Mr. Cole will not look forward to it either."

"Alright," Stone said. "So what's the thing about tips?"

"The negotiations are for your wages. That is and always will be paid in gold. If the client wishes to suggest other forms of payment, let him know that Sinanju only receives gold as a wage, but other forms of payment are acceptable as tribute to the individual master."

"We get tips?" Stone asked. "Unbelievable."

"Sinanju created tipping," Sunny Joe said. "Our first tip came from Mu."

"Moo?" Stone asked. "Like...cow talk? 'Moo?'"

"No, Stone. 'Mu,' not 'moo.' This was before the Sun Source, before Wang. The entire civilization of Mu disappeared into the sea," Sunny Joe began and then hesitated. "No, that is too long of a lesson for now. I will tell you about Mu on your return."

"What?" Stone asked. "Wait a minute! You mean you're gonna stop telling the one tale of the past Masters that actually sounds interesting? Was it Atlantis?"

Sunny Joe ignored the question and sat down, crossing his legs. He motioned for Stone and Freya to do likewise. They sat down in front of Sunny Joe, adopting his sitting position. Stone cringed.

It is morning.

All is calm.

I stand beside a flower.

It is a great flower, green of stem and leaf.

Oh, see the great flower, blessed with many petals.

Oh, see golden petals, which surround the flower like a halo!

Oh, soft and golden petals, frail and beautiful, I salute you!

The northern petal greets me.

The northeastern petal greets me.

The eastern petal greets me.

The southeastern petal greets me.

The southern petal greets me.

The southwestern petal greets me.

The western petal greets me.

The northwestern petal greets me.

The flower bows in the wind in graceful salute…

One hour into the reading, Sunny Joe ignored Stone's artificial cough.

Stone did not want him to ignore the cough.

"We know the poem, grandpa," Stone said. "This is supposed to torture our clients, not us!"

Sunny Joe only moved his eyes Stone's way and Stone shrank back down into position.

"Okay," Stone mumbled. "Sorry."

Sunny Joe closed his eyes and continued.

Stone closed his eyes and wished it were over.

In the middle of the field, I see a bee.

It is a grand bee.

How delicate the wings of this bee!

The hair on his legs finer than silk!

His very flight produces songs of buzzing!

Oh, bee, see the flower with the golden petals?

The northern petal greets the bee.

The northeastern petal greets the bee.

The eastern petal greets the bee.

The southeastern petal greets the bee.

The southern petal greets the bee.

The southwestern petal greets the bee.

The western petal greets the bee.

The northwestern petal greets the bee.

The flower bows in the wind in graceful salute.

The bee swirls in tribute to the grace of the flower.

Beautiful flower, behold the bee!

Petals, sisters one and all, defender of the flower, accept the

bee!

The bee swirls in tribute to the power of the petals.

The great bee performs the pollen dance!

The bee dances amidst the pollen.

The flower observes the sun.

The sun observes the flower.

The bee observes the sun.

The sun observes the bee.

Another hour later, Stone fidgeted out of his lotus position. Just thinking about taking a smoke break was causing him to rub his fingers together. Sunny Joe ignored his nervousness, continuing about the beauty of the air surrounding the bee. Stone closed his eyes and exhaled.

"Okay, okay, we get it!" Stone said, throwing his hands up. "The whole world is beautiful! Birds, bees, the clouds—they are all beautiful! Zippity-doo-dah! Can't we just...Ow!"

Sunny Joe held his fingernail at the top of Stone's spine, freezing him and his voice.

"The morning wind surrounds them all..." Sunny Joe continued, ignoring the pleading look on his grandson's face.

CHAPTER SIX

Monica Hill had started working at Kumar's Restaurant almost twenty years ago. She washed dishes before she finally became a waitress. Primarily a breakfast bar, the restaurant had served the St. Louis suburb of Wood River for just as long. It was the type of place that was established with the residents, and it was rare for someone Monica did not know to walk through the doors. So when four men decked out like lumberjacks, complete with plaid shirts and blue jeans entered the door, it caught her attention. She was not aware of anyone logging on the Illinois side of St. Louis. She grabbed four menus, but stopped in front of the grill where her friend Trish was cooking.

"Something's weird about those guys," Monica said.

"You mean four men coming in here by themselves? Yeah, that's weird," Trish said, rolling her eyes.

"That's not what I meant!" Monica whispered loudly. "They just rub me the wrong way."

"You just better check for a wedding ring before they try to rub you the right way," Trish said, winking. "The tall one's pretty cute."

"Hush," Monica said, walking to the table.

The men were leaning closely together whispering when she approached. The tall one was sketching something on a piece of paper. When he saw Monica, he folded the paper and stuck it in his pocket. All four men looked up at her with friendly smiles.

"Morning, guys. My name is Monica and I'll be your server today. We have everything from pancakes and sausage to donuts and our famous all-you-can-drink coffee. So, what can I get you?"

"Well, Monica, my name's Robert," the tallest man said. His smile was contagious. "And honey, you can start by bringing me and the boys some of your famous coffee."

Monica avoided the other men's glances and fought back a blush. As a mother of four in her mid-forties, it had been years since men looked at her that way. Any suspicions she had were quickly buried in their flattery.

And that was exactly how Robert had planned it. He was the commander of Tech Force, the Secret Service computer branch of the National Security Administration.

"So why did they send you?" the man known as Estefan asked Robert. Robert directed Tech Force projects, and usually only showed on site if something was wrong. "This is a big project, but we got it under control. This project rub you the wrong way?"

"I'm here because I was told to be here. That decision is far above your pay grade," Robert replied, looking at the menu.

"Well, I think this job is dangerous," Estefan continued. "Think about it. After we finish this job, every scrap of processed information in the northern hemisphere is gonna run through this hub."

"And?" Robert asked. "That's why they want the upgrade."

"That's too much power in one location," Estefan said. He lowered his voice as Monica returned with coffee.

"Not my call," Robert said, smiling.

While Monica filled their coffee cups and took their orders, the men changed the topic to Cardinals baseball, but as soon as she left, Estefan leaned close to Robert.

"We're setting up infinite power to an operative who is described as 'Middle-Eastern descent' and that doesn't raise a red flag for you?"

"You a racist, Estefan?"

"I'm a realist."

"Anyone else here a realist?" Robert asked. "Bert?"

"I do what I'm told. Nothing I could do anyway."

What about you, Zak? You have an opinion?"

The table turned to look at the youngest member of the squad. Robert could tell he was itching to put his two cents in.

"Everyone should have an opinion about national security," Zak said. "It helps keeps us honest."

"You obviously haven't been working for the company very long," Robert said. "So speak up."

"Our orders could have been faked," Zak said. "It's happened before."

"Are you saying that we should disobey our orders?"

"Of course not," Zak said. "I'm just saying that we follow our orders with open eyes. If this guy doesn't seem kosher, I say we take him out, or at least bug out before we do the job."

"That's the easy solution, isn't it?" Robert noted. "That way you don't have to engage your brain and think. I'll keep my eye on the contact as we perform the work *we were ordered to do*. If our contact does not appear to be who we have been told, I will personally take him out. But until then, just remember, he has rank. You three are the throwaways here."

The men remained mostly quiet for the remainder of their breakfast, changing the conversation as necessary. Monica had come by twice to refill Robert's cup, but thought nothing more of the men. When they left the restaurant, they left a big tip and passed the small bar on the corner, turning left to a tax preparation office. The front door had a small sign that read "See you next tax season."

Robert pulled out his cell phone and sent a text as the other three fanned out on the sidewalk standing guard. The confirmation text was almost immediate and he unlocked the front door. The other three walked backwards into the front door, keeping an eye on their surroundings. Once inside, they left the lights out and removed the small jackets they wore. The briefcases and satchels they carried were opened and automatic pistols were handed out to each man. Estefan entered the door code to the manager's office and entered. The other three followed, one by one.

Robert sent another coded text and a small click filled the manager's office. The other men slid the desk to the side and pulled back the rug, revealing a hatch. Robert opened the hatch and two others followed him down the spiral staircase. Estefan closed the flooring behind them, sliding the desk back in place. He took a seat behind the desk with his loaded pistol in his lap. Anyone entering the office would be shot.

The three men exited the elevator, entering a small chamber.

"Tobacco Mountain," Robert said to the intercom microphone.

The door clicked open and Robert and his men entered. Inside the large air-conditioned room were the computers that had been installed over the last two months. To avoid suspicion, most of the parts had been brought in a few at a time by different teams, and installed incrementally.

One man stood in the midst of the computers. He appeared to be a middle-aged man of average height and weight, with dark, thick hair and a carefully trimmed beard.

And he was of Middle Eastern descent, just as headquarters had said.

Ben Cole noted that only three men exited the elevator. His order had called for four.

Robert did not need to know Ben's name any more than he needed to know Robert's. Each man was there for their own purposes and their own orders. Each would guard their secrets. Without hesitation or remorse, Robert walked to Ben and pointed his pistol at Ben's forehead.

"What year is it?" he asked. Ben would have one chance to correctly answer, or Robert would pull the trigger and return in one week after the place had been swept clean.

"September," Ben replied in a slightly tinted accent. Robert holstered his pistol. "I checked the network before you arrived," Ben said. "All security gates are confirmed."

"We are going to re-confirm them," Robert said, keeping his eye on Ben.

"The order was for four men," Ben said.

"I don't do this level of work without at least one man on guard duty. If you wanted four techs, you should have ordered five men. You have a problem with that?"

"I have a problem with orders not being followed."

"Orders were followed. You asked for four men, and four men came. If you don't like it, then file a complaint," Robert said. "We're gonna start working."

Ben stood back to let the men have access to the computers. Without a fourth man working on the installation, the job was going to take longer than he had planned.

"Start with comm one," Robert ordered.

Each of the men hooked up their small tablets to the computer in front of them. When one was through, another would follow behind to confirm his work. They repeated the procedure on all four computers. It took over six hours for the men to confirm the security.

Ben followed behind them, watching them put the security through its paces. No matter what protocol they tried, the gate shut down their attempts to hack the system. The computers performed better than he had hoped.

Robert walked up to Ben and handed him a small key.

"This will allow you access once a month and no more. Every time this key is used, it will be recorded at Langley. Use it in any way that it is not designed to be used and I'll be back."

Ben was aware of the security protocols, since he had personally designed them. Robert was correct in not spelling them out, though. If the key was misused, the elevator would freeze between floors, and cyanide gas would pump inside, killing the occupant. But Robert gave Ben the key believing that he needed it to access the computer room.

Robert was wrong.

"We will be in contact in four months," Robert said. "Don't change anything."

The men left and Ben waited for the elevator to come to a complete halt before turning to one of the computers. He hooked his cell phone to one of the ports and punched a few buttons. His phone displayed the hidden cameras scattered in a four-block radius of his base. Ben followed the men as they left the building, each leaving in separate, nondescript rental cars.

The men thought that Ben was supposed to follow them up the elevator ten minutes after they left, and sealed the elevator as a final safeguard. If Ben had been an imposter, he would not have the timed codes to exit the facility, and when Robert and his team returned in four months, they would find his lifeless body in the midst of the new computers.

They need not have worried.

Ben tapped two separate places on the frame of the elevator door. The elevator did not come down, but the door opened and Ben turned to the left side of the shaft. He pulled back one of the old, worn-out looking plates. As he did, the door shut behind him and the elevator slowly began to descend. He had twenty seconds to enter the proper code or the elevator would crush him.

Ben entered the code, the side panel opened, and he stepped back into his office. The door shut behind him before the elevator dropped and Ben headed for his desk. He rebooted his computer, ready to test the new system capabilities.

The new computer screen was a series of tiles, each specifying a custom task. SECURITY. NEWS. SEARCHES. ANALYSIS. He clicked on SECURITY and the monitors placed around the top of the wall began displaying his office from the inside out, though the elevator, upstairs into the hallway and the inside of Mike's Bar, as well as all of the custom high definition traffic cameras placed at every stop light within a six-block radius.

Ben smiled.

He went upstairs and, finding Mike alone, sat at the bar. The large man who was guardian to his bunker fit the model of a stereotypical bar owner. Mike carried a presence that Ben was sure had to be part of his real personality.

"Vodka gimlet," Ben said.

Mike grabbed a glass and began pouring vodka. He grabbed a small green plastic bottle and squirted some lime juice into the glass and began stirring it.

"You still on the clock?" Mike asked, placing a slice of lime on the side of the glass.

"I'm always on the clock," Ben answered. "How's the new system?"

"It's gonna take some time to get used to the new layout," Mike said. "It's gotta be better than the old system they had in place."

"We'll run trials tomorrow," Ben said, taking a sip of his drink. "We don't want to accidentally blow the entire city block up."

"Five bucks," Mike said.

Ben slipped him a ten and carried his drink back downstairs. "Night," Ben said.

"Hey," Mike shouted. "Don't forget to bring my glass back!"

CHAPTER SEVEN

Stone and Freya left the training hut later in the afternoon. Stone rubbed his neck and coughed, trying to get his voice back. His throat felt so raw that he did not even feel like smoking.

"You should be back to normal in a few hours," Freya said. "I'm familiar with the technique Grandfather used."

"Can't you fix it, then?" Stone asked with a low rasp.

"Since I cannot center, I don't have the precise control needed to manipulate your nerve clusters. If I tried right now, I could very well cripple you."

"You said that you can center for short periods."

"I also said that it produces intense pain, which is why I cannot retain my center."

"Crap," Stone murmured, trying to clear his throat. "There is no way I'm going to survive four hours of Ung poetry,"

"I think that's the point," Freya said. "If you would just look at it as a thrust or a stroke, it fits."

"Okay, when you're able to center again, you're handling the Ung," Stone said. "Behold, Freya Williams, Reigning Mistress of Ung Poetry!"

"I will be glad to once I am able to center again," Freya said. "I feel that I can never quite catch my breath."

"I'm going to try to run for a bit, and see if that helps," Stone said, breathing slowly and deeply.

Freya watched the process as Stone bent slightly backward to grab a deep breath. She knew that his lungs were expanding to increase efficiency. She knew that energy was flooding his body to the point he could perform superhuman feats. Stone grinned and waved at Freya before bolting off into the distance at full Sinanju speed. It looked to Freya as if he was standing beside her, and then he was suddenly far away, at the end of a long dust cloud. Grandfather said that training badly resulted in bad training, but Freya would not tell him about the dust cloud Stone had left behind.

Freya began to walk home, pausing in front of the general store. *Since her body was not able to center, would she be able to eat non-Sinanju kosher food again?* It had been weeks since she had last eaten chocolate! For more than a moment, she was tempted to see if she could try a bite, but Sunny Joe's words came back to haunt her. Sure, she might be able to find a few more compatible foods, but what if she ended up dead? Her life wasn't worth chocolate...*even if it was sweet and delicious*...she shook her head and banished the thought from her mind. The moment of weakness passed and she turned toward home when a figure approached her from behind.

Freya swung around, ready to strike, when she recognized Tekoa. He stepped back, holding his hands up.

"Whoa! I just wanted to say hi!" he said.

Freya relaxed her stance.

"I'm sorry, my mind is wandering," she said, embarrassed. She was not used to someone being able to sneak up on her. "Can I help you?"

"Just wanted to say I'm sorry about the other day at the basketball court. The guys were being jerks."

"That is their way," Freya said. "One day they will go too far."

"Don't tell him that I told you, but you know that Tommy likes you, right? That's what he acts that way."

"He certainly does not know how to show it," Freya said and then frowned. "At one time, I liked him as well."

"I wanted to tell you something," Tekoa said nervously.

"Yes?" Freya asked. She was not in the mood to talk to anyone, but Tekoa had been kind to her.

Tekoa looked down for a few seconds and then looked back into her eyes. That is when he noticed her eyes were a soft purple, unlike any eyes he had seen before.

"Hmmm," he mused. "I've never seen purple eyes before."

"They are common among my mother's people," Freya said. "I am sorry, but I need to leave. We have to be up early to catch a flight."

"I just wanted you to know that I asked Sunny Joe if I could be a member of your tribe," Tekoa said. "What do you think?"

"I cannot speak for my grandfather, but this is a wonderful place. Good people live here."

"Guess I haven't seen many of the good people yet. Most people treat me like a disease."

"Grandfather let us move here and we still get stares. You see how I am treated."

"Yeah, but you guys kinda have the genetic lottery going for you on that one," Tekoa said. "No one is gonna turn away their own grandchildren."

"Perhaps, but he is a fair man."

"Let's hope so. Have a good flight," Tekoa said. "See you when you get back?"

"Sure," Freya said.

Freya entered the only store on the small reservation. She sighed as the others inside began staring at her. Since her body had changed during the Night of the Salt, her diet had been reduced to a very select group of foods. She could not handle processed foods of any kind, nor anything with additives — even sugar or salt. Turning her head to avoid looking at the selection of candy bars, she walked straight to the aisle reserved for Sunny

Joe, sighing as she picked up a few ears of corn and a slab of walleye fish.

Not being able to center and still being held to a Sinanju diet really sucked.

CHAPTER EIGHT

Jonathan Hilgiver had never felt as if he belonged. He was the middle of five children in an upper-class Boston family. He could never fit in at his large school, and could never seem to keep, or even make, any friends. He graduated in the middle of his class without distinction, without ambition, without drive—without a connection of any kind. He never felt the need to prove himself to others. His mediocrity came with an especially strong sense of arrogance: he believed that he was own unique species—a different, better species of human.

To others, however, he simply appeared rude and standoffish, and they treated him accordingly. Most people kept their taunting whispers out of hearing range or behind barely concealed looks of disgust, but a few took pleasure in putting Jonathan in his place. They never wanted to let him forget that he was not one of them, and would never be one of them.

He had all but withdrawn from humanity by the time he was in fourth grade, reserving his anger for those things that could not strike back. One summer day, on his way back from the library, he saw an injured bird on a sidewalk. It was still alive, but could hardly move. A few ants were already skittering across the bird's body and Jonathan stopped to lean over. He smiled as he softly nudged the bird closer to the anthill with his foot. He came back in a few minutes with a hamburger and soda and sat down next to the anthill to watch the bird slowly die.

Things quickly progressed to larger animals, especially pets of those whom he hated. And then, one day, soon after graduating high school, he began to look at small children the same way he looked at animals. He realized that they were not fully human yet. They were just biological sponges, waiting for the software of the masses to be implanted so they could become drones like the rest of their kind. Keeping them from growing into cubicle-bound zombies would be, in Jonathan's opinion, an act of mercy, like drowning deformed kittens after birth.

Jonathan was first arrested when he was twenty after abducting a small girl on her way home from school. Though the policeman handcuffed Jonathan and tossed him in the back of his patrol car, he did not drive to the station for processing. Instead, the policeman drove outside of the city and, for a few terrifying minutes, Jonathan believed that the policeman was going to kill him. The officer would not even make eye contact with Jonathan.

The policeman pulled over on a country road, next to a small van, and opened the door.

"Take him before I change my mind," the policeman said.

Jonathan could not see who he was speaking to, but the driver handed the policeman some money. The car door opened and

Jonathan felt himself being pulled out of the back. He was slammed against the car and the cuffs were removed. Before he could move, the policeman placed his pistol at the back of Jonathan's head.

He heard the hammer being cocked.

"That was my cousin's little girl you took. If you ever come back to my city again, you're a dead man," he said. "Do you understand me?"

Jonathan could barely nod his head yes for fear of making the policeman accidentally pull the trigger. When the policeman left, Jonathan noticed that he had soiled himself.

"I have been looking for you," a soft voice said from inside the van.

Jonathan slowly moved toward the front, only to see an old man dressed in a long dark jacket. He had a scraggly beard and happy eyes. Jonathan recognized happy eyes. He hated happy eyes.

"Why do you allow yourself to be bound by rules that others obey like mindless cattle? We are not like them, you and I."

His voice, now louder, carried an accent. Jonathan could not recognize it; the accent could have belonged to any of a dozen nations.

"Do not be ashamed," the man said. "You no longer have a reason to hide."

The man's beard parted for a toothy smile and though

Jonathan did not trust this man—he did not trust anyone—there was something about him that made Jonathan listen.

Over the next two weeks, the man showed Jonathan the way.

Jonathan heard the man as if no one else had ever talked to him in his entire life. He had finally found someone who understood what it meant to be different, and who showed Jonathan what it was to *belong* somewhere. From that moment forth, the man said that he would no longer be called by a name he did not choose. The man helped Jonathan pick out a new name for his new life, and Jasir ibn Abdullah was born.

Once he passed his studies, he was taken to a new home in Galveston, Texas. The men he met were others who thought like him, and who were apathetic to the trivial desires of the human condition. The authorities had tried to label some of them as psychopathic, but the man who led them was not a psychopath, though he knew that he could band them together into an unstoppable force.

After two years, the group grew too large to remain in one place. Jasir took control of the Galveston group while his leader took the rest of the group to Ohio.

Jasir began transporting goods and soldiers to various parts of America. When the infidels were attacked on September 11, Jasir just *knew* that his cell was to be called next, but they were merely told to wait.

Time passed and Jasir and his men continued to blend into

their communities, but something would not settle in Jasir's heart. He had made several radical connections over the years, but had not managed to make a name for himself. But one day, following orders to transport a package to a remote area, everything changed.

As Jasir arrived, he saw smoke in the distance. When he drove more closely, he could see the building that was his destination had been burnt down. He stopped a quarter-mile away to see the still-smoldering building push black smoke into the sky when he heard the jingle of a cell phone in the back of the van. He then heard a sharp grunt as if someone had been punched. Ignoring his orders not to pass through the curtain separating him from the back, Jasir pulled over and saw a woman lying on the floor of the van with a knife protruding from her chest. Her eyes lazily focused on him as she coughed up blood. A dagger fell out of her right hand while a flash drive fell out of her left.

His phone received a one-word text: ABORT.

Jasir knew what that meant. He left the woman to bleed to death in the back and drove the van deep into the countryside, setting fire to both van and woman.

But he kept the flash drive.

When he returned to his base, he found several top-secret documents on the flash drive, including plans on taking out the majority of America's power grid.

Jasir had found his way to serve.

He began throwing out queries to his underground contacts. He would find a way to use the information, to take down the country that had broken him. He would beat them into the dirt until the ants skittered across their corpses.

A few people had shown interest in his project, but when the infamous Marcus Eames asked for an audience to exchange information and weaponry, Jasir quickly agreed. He did not know that his contacts were at the level of someone such as Eames.

The thought of kidnapping Marcus and claiming the million-dollar bounty on the infamous spy briefly crossed Jasir's mind, but he knew that Eames' information was worth far more than money. He also knew that everyone who had tried to take down Eames had suffered a quick, violent death.

Eames' reputation was as a ruthless trader of knowledge. He would always deliver a good bargain and never showed hostility unless he was attacked. To date, everyone who had ever attacked him had failed or died.

Jasir's makeshift base was an abandoned elementary school, built during the Cold War, complete with a small nuclear shelter below. They had taken over the building long after anyone lived in the neighborhood and painted all of the windows in the gym to hide their presence.

Eames arrived on time in a modest sedan and pulled around to the gym entrance. Despite his men's apprehension, Jasir had ordered them to show Eames respect as if he were a foreign dignitary. He was not frisked at the door like an airport security check. Rifles were even lowered as Marcus walked by the front door.

* * *

Lax security at the gate, Eames thought, taking note of his surroundings.

Sentries are overweight, holding weapons awkwardly, most likely inexperienced.

Security cameras aimed away from points of entry, indicating no one monitoring the premises.

* * *

Jasir's lieutenant greeted Eames with a warm smile and a rattling cough. He led Eames directly to Jasir in the school gym. Jasir sat behind a scoreboard table on the side of the gym in an old wooden chair. The place had obviously never been cleaned since they took over.

* * *

Second-in-command is unarmed. Has breathing troubles and a painful limp. Threat level is low.

Dust reveals one path of footprints leading from front

entryway to gym to only the door on the right. No one else in either of the other two doors.

* * *

"Hello, my brother," Eames greeted, opening both arms for a hug. Jasir, normally cautious about bodily contact, continued to hold his fake smile and returned the hug. He felt Eames's famed bulletproof coat and the telltale bulge of a pistol under his side. Jasir assumed it was Eames' way of politely informing him that he was armed.

"What can my mighty band of men do for the great Marcus Eames?"

"I need your help," Marcus said quietly, as if he were confiding a great secret. "I've heard that you have a plan to sabotage the American electric grid."

Jasir cocked his head cautiously. While he had sought access to arms and cooperation with others, he had never mentioned the electrical grid in any of his queries. He unconsciously turned his gaze toward the men he suspected of talking. His face was devoid of a smile when he returned to look at Marcus.

"This is not something I am prepared to discuss yet," Jasir said. "There are many preparations still to come. Perhaps there is something else you would like?"

"No, Jasir, this is what I have come to discuss. Should you be unwilling to discuss, I shall leave," Marcus said as he quickly rose from his chair.

"Wait," Jasir said. A contact like Marcus could not be easily abandoned. If it meant that he had to expedite his plans, so be it. "Let us discuss."

Marcus smiled graciously as he returned to his seat. "Thank you, Jasir. Now let me be direct—from what I have heard, you plan to take out fifty percent of America's power grids?"

"Sixty percent!" Jasir said, proudly correcting him.

Marcus held up his hand.

"Grids can be fixed, Jasir. What you must do instead is to shut down the power plants themselves," Marcus said in a soft voice. Leaning forward conspiratorially, he added "What if I told you of a way that you could shut down *all* of America's power plants, including the nuclear plants, and trick the CIA into doing it themselves?"

Jasir looked up in thought. "Is such an act possible?"

"Yes. What matters is their response. If an electrical grid simply fails, they can fix it quickly. More importantly, they can send in many men to hunt you down, and you will die in vain. But if the government believes that restoring power to a grid will threaten national security, they would rather the area stay dark for days—weeks, even—rather than threaten their beloved populace."

Jasir nodded. "But how do we convince them of the threat we pose?"

"This government is crippled by cowardice and bureaucracy, Jasir, and you must learn to use that to your advantage. Once you learn their 'official' response to a threat such as this, you will have complete control over their actions. Think of the possibility: you and your men will be credited with shutting down the Great Satan, and you will be alive to hear the praise."

Jasir's eyes squinted as his mouth stretched in a toothy grin.

"We are to be good friends, you and I," Jasir said. "What could you possibly need from us in return?"

"The codes you already have for the electrical grids," Marcus said. "I have a buyer for them."

"What good will the codes be after I have shut down the Great Satan?"

"My buyers don't know that. They hired me to get the codes from you. If you shut down the power before they get a chance to do so, that is their problem. And this way, we shall all profit."

Dropping his voice, he continued. "Do you have a place where we can talk further?" Marcus asked. "You obviously have a few...indiscriminate soldiers."

Jasir looked around.

"I did not choose these men," Jasir admitted. "They are sometimes...too excited for their own good. Let us continue in my office," he said, gesturing to what had once been the principal's office.

Jasir led Marcus through a set of swinging double doors,

down a small hallway, and into the office. A faded sticker, proclaiming that the previous occupant had "put the 'pal' in 'principal'" still clung to the door. As soon both men were inside and the door was closed, Marcus spun Jasir around, and struck him in the back of the head. Jasir's head smashed downward, into the doorknob. Marcus took Jasir's pistol from its holster, and kicked him in the solar plexus. Jasir collapsed to the floor.

Casually gliding back into the gym, Marcus smiled at the guards. "Jasir said that he needs your help moving some stuff."

All three guards began walking towards the hallway.

The oldest guard is the largest threat, Marcus noted, after the man refused to take his eyes off him.

As the double doors swung open, Marcus pulled two slender knives from inside his coat. He lunged at the oldest guard and spun, slicing his jugular before anyone had a chance to reach for their weapons. The guard reached for his throat and Marcus grabbed his rifle, striking him in the forehead.

It took the other two a moment to process what was happening before reaching for their own rifles. Marcus leapt over the dead man and shot the larger of the two remaining guards in the teeth, spattering blood on the final guard. The young man had managed to raise his rifle, but Marcus was already beside him. He placed the muzzle into the man's face and pulled the trigger once.

The sound of shouts and stomping feet came from behind the gym, but Marcus was already hidden behind the bleachers by the time they entered. Seeing their fallen comrades in the doorway, the men ran toward them, thinking Marcus was behind the doors. A small tap of the fully automatic rifle Marcus had taken removed that mistaken perception.

Only Jasir's second-in-command was unaccounted for. Marcus knew that he would either try to arm himself and attack, or, if he were smart, he would flee.

Marcus sprinted back to the principal's office, but Jasir was not there.

Jasir staggered down the long concrete tunnel that had been constructed during the Cold War to shelter children in case of a nuclear attack. He wiped the blood from his face, vowing eternal vengeance on Marcus Eames.

"I shall hire more men and place a jihad on Eames," he thought. *"The Great Satan can wait."*

The shots above him stopped and Jasir hurried his pace. When they took over the school as their base, Jasir had hidden both ends of the shelter tunnel. On the inside entrance, they nailed a bunch of boards to the front of the door leading to the tunnel. To a casual glance, it appeared that the door was nailed shut to the wall. The metal hatch outside was covered with fully-grown bushes and impossible to detect unless you knew where it was. Jasir took a deep breath as he reached the other end of the tunnel. The exit door was near, but he was still seeing stars.

Jasir would have the doctors look at him. There was no telling what damage Eames had caused with his brutish attack. Eames's reputation as a peaceful trader of information would be revealed as the falsehood it was. Jasir pulled the hatch lever on the reinforced exit door, but it did not budge. He leaned in and pushed harder. The door opened just enough for him to see a chain securing the door from the outside.

He was locked in.

"I do my homework," Marcus said at the other end of the tunnel. "But to be quite honest, you're so stupid that I didn't have to do much."

"How dare you!" Jasir shouted impotently. "You are...*nothing*! A mere peddler!"

Marcus ignored his babbling and pulled a small folder from inside his jacket. Jasir immediately recognized the file and mindlessly reached for his jacket pocket, but it was not there. The folder was the one piece of information he could not leave behind. It contained notes of everything he planned to do.

And now Marcus Eames held the folder, as if he owned it.

"Speaking of information, this was the only thing of value I could find in the entire place and I pulled that from your jacket when we first met."

Incensed with rage, Jasir pulled a curved blade from the side of his tunic. The blade was specially made to produce cuts that would not heal.

"Are these all of your plans?" Marcus asked. His voice clearly did not register Jasir as a threat.

"Die!" Jasir screamed, slashing wildly at Marcus through the narrow gap in the door.

Marcus stared at the bloody figure as if he were watching a sunset. Jasir led with his knife, but Marcus was already moving with him. Marcus parried, violently slapping the blade from his hand and punched Jasir in the jaw, knocking him to the floor. Marcus picked up the curved knife and stabbed Jasir in the left shoulder, twisting the blade until it broke off inside the bone. He tossed the handle away and placed his hand over the wound.

Jasir's mouth opened, but no sound came out.

"That was a nice blade," Marcus said calmly. "A wound like that won't heal."

Jasir began to scream, but Marcus slapped him hard across the face with his free hand. "Jasir, focus. I am the only thing keeping you alive right now and I need you to listen."

Jasir tried to spit at Marcus, but Marcus merely stepped to the side and slapped him again.

"Are these all of your plans?" he asked.

Jasir tried to curse, but Marcus grabbed his arm and twisted it behind his back. The hallway filled with Jasir's screams. Over the next twelve minutes, with his last breaths, he gave Marcus all of the information he wanted and more.

And then Marcus bent his arm upward until he heard a thick crack. Lights exploded in the back of Jasir's eyes and he collapsed to the floor unconscious. Marcus searched him, finding only a small flash drive. Marcus set off a few incendiary grenades near the center of the school. He was miles away when the building finally collapsed in on itself, an ancient and fiery hulk.

CHAPTER NINE

The Sinanju tribe had never had a hospital. Most of the injuries and sicknesses were treated by Ike Hodges, the tribe's only doctor. Doc Hodges was a resident of two worlds. Though his father trained him to follow his footsteps to take over as the next tribal shaman, Ike was also a graduate of UCLA's medical school.

He was also on the very short list of people Sunny Joe counted as true friends.

Though two decades his junior, Sunny Joe was happy to see Doc Hodges drag the Sinanju into the twentieth century. He was a bit short on bedside manner, but most of the time, Doc Hodges knew what to do. For the most part, he would just give his patients time to rant and then he would prescribe a placebo. He very quickly realized the similarity of the shamanistic ceremonies that 'infused magic' into whatever elixir was given to the patient and modern procedures to providing medicine.

First, he would glance out the window of his small office as if he were making sure no one was watching and then he would remove a small orange bottle of sugar pills from his top right drawer full of orange bottles of sugar pills. Before he handed it to his patient, he warned them not to take more than one a day. The patient would leave and Doc's magic—new magic, he called it—worked wonders.

But a few patients had real problems that were not so easily fixed by placebos. Dale had beat cancer in his fifties, but it had showed up again last year. Sunny Joe tried to tell Dale that he could smell it, but Dale balked about following up, partly because he did not want to face the problem, but mostly because he did not believe one could smell cancer. He thought it was Sunny Joe's way of getting him to visit the doctor. But when the pain started, Dale knew that Sunny Joe was right. Only when Sunny Joe ordered Dale to see the Doc or be replaced by his son did Dale actually make an appointment.

Doc Hodge's building was as near to the center of the reservation without being a part of the original main street buildings. It was a modest metal building, originally designed for schools, but was spacious enough for Doc to care of his patients.

Sunny Joe entered and Doc smiled.

"What ails you today, Sunny Joe?" Doc asked. He knew that Sunny Joe's health was better than his own, despite being two decades younger.

"Too many things that medicine can't cure," Sunny Joe said, sitting down. "I'm just checking to make sure Dale showed up and see if there is anything I can do."

"Of course, outside the reservation, doctor/client

confidentiality would prohibit me from saying anything," Doc said, as he did every time Sunny Joe asked about someone from the tribe. "But, between us, Dale is pretty sick. I advised him to seek treatment at a cancer center, but he's determined to get treated locally or not at all."

"He is definitely a stubborn man," Sunny Joe said.

"If his body were as stubborn as his mind, he would never get sick."

"What's your diagnosis?"

"Not good. I am very limited in what I can do in this office. I've given him some of my dad's herbal tea and a few pain medications, but as far as I can tell, he's only drinking the tea."

"I wouldn't even count on that," Sunny Joe said, shaking his head. "Is there anything you could do to…improve your daddy's recipe?"

"With prescription medicine? Oh, it's far too late for that. He needs serious therapy and I can't provide that on the reservation."

"What should he do?" Sunny Joe asked.

"Check himself in to a cancer treatment facility. Yesterday."

"Guess it's time for me to pull rank."

"If you want to celebrate Dale's next birthday, you had better."

Sunny Joe thought for a moment. It really would not hurt anything other than tradition to teach Dale the basic breathing technique. If Dale were able to master basic breathing, it would fuel his cells and make them strong enough to heal his cancer. It was not as if Sunny Joe was going to train Dale in Sinanju and compete with the House.

But if anyone ever found out that Sunny Joe had broken another of the tribe's primary laws, it would give Paul Moore an excuse to try to have Sunny Joe removed. And even though Chiun, the master of the Korean House of Sinanju was strangely accepting of the fact that Sunny Joe was training Freya, Sunny Joe did not wish to push his luck with Chiun—doing so would only earn him an immediate, one-way ticket to his own funeral.

"Sunny Joe, get Dale the help he needs. Turtle paste and placebos aren't going to keep him alive," Doc said softly.

CHAPTER TEN

In the 1960s, when the CIA constructed "Mike's Bar," it was a time when 'secrecy' and 'military' were words that no one questioned. Mike's not only concealed one of the most comprehensive Presidential bunkers ever built, the bar was purposely built far off the beaten path in a small Illinois hamlet just outside St. Louis. While the menu touted four columns of mixed drinks and the bar itself always carried ample bowls of pretzels, Mike's true commodity was privacy. Officials were able to conduct top-secret negotiations and trade deals far from the prying eyes of Beltway reporters and pesky sub-committees.

Mike's opulent interior more than made up for the drab exterior. The designers had installed a custom horseshoe-shaped mahogany bar, complete with solid brass rails. Full-grain leather seats surrounded the bar. The dining tables were solid teakwood with gold-leaf inlays. Tiffany glass chandeliers dangled above each table. Even the floor was hand-scraped wood for an old-world feel.

The first 'Mike' was appointed to run the bar for the last two years before his retirement, and he served all the great Cold War spies, from MI6 to Mossad. He had even hosted a former Soviet spy once or twice. The first 'Mike' loved the assignment so much that he overstayed his post eight years. They had to force him into retirement to make room for the next 'Mike'.

As technology made face-to-face meetings among intelligence agents a thing of the past, Mike's Bar was used less frequently over the years. As the latest Mike to run the bar looked around, very little of the glory days remained. The wooden flooring had begun to warp from age and lack of care. The original hand-scraped texture had long ago been buried beneath layers of cheap wax and floor polish. The fine leather seats had been replaced in the nineties with cost-effective plastic-topped barstools. The stained-glass chandeliers were sold and replaced with fluorescent lights.

The only thing that remained was the Monster. That's what the current Mike called the bulletproof mahogany bar that stood in the center of the main room. Through its fifty-year history, it had withstood everything: fights, spills, clumsy patrons, and, during one particularly tense evening, five shots from a 9mm handgun.

Mike wiped down the Monster and slid the beer to an old man at the end of the bar. Surprisingly, nothing spilled. The old man who grabbed the beer was Patch Edwards, a retired Colonel from the Australian Air Force. For a few years, Patch worked alongside the CIA. Legends of Mike's Bar were still floating around when he was in the service. Patch made sure to put it on his bucket list.

For the past three weeks, he had been the bar's only regular patron.

"Now *that's* how you're supposed to serve beer, mate!" Patch said, his smile revealing only three teeth.

Mike smiled and joined him at the end of the bar.

"Don't count on me doing that all the time," Mike said. "If I spill it, you're buying a new one."

"Money I got, Mike," Patch said and then the smile drained from his craggy face. "The thing I've been running out of is friends. You ever get someone drop by from the glory days?"

"Nah, but I've only had the bar a year. In fact, I had no idea that this place even had a claim to fame until you showed up and I still don't know whether to believe you or not. I really just bought it because it was already named Mike's," Mike lied.

In fact, just about everything other than Mike's first name was a lie. To Patch and other inquisitive bar guests, Mike Nelson was a retired steel worker who had purchased the bar after his wife left him. In reality, he was Michael Clemmons, a covert gatekeeper protecting one of the most secret agencies in American history. Mike was the eighth owner of the bar. He had been assigned the bar after the last 'Mike' retired.

Unlike the heady years of the sixties and seventies, Mike did not have to arrange secret meetings or cater specialty meals. Unlike the original Mike, he did not have a full kitchen staff or a gourmet chef. He had beer, liquor, and the Monster.

His job was very simple: if anyone came in who seemed

suspicious, Mike would tap the alarm, notifying Ben Cole. The alarm would freeze the elevators and if necessary, Mike would kill the intruder. If he were successful, he would send the code to Ben, who would have the option of unlocking the elevators, or detonating the explosives that lined the block. The resulting explosion would tear a hole in the middle of the town, killing hundreds of people. The explosion would be blamed on a faulty gas line. The paperwork had already been prepared, showing that the mayor had ignored years of complaints from his city planning department.

Hundreds of lives and one political career was a cheap price for keeping the President's bunker beneath the bar a secret.

"So I'm your first famous visitor?" Patch asked, smiling.

"I guess so, Patch. And hey, you've got it made. You get to travel all over the world, see the sights. No curfew…you can sleep in 'til noon if you want!"

"Really? So, when are *you* gonna retire?" Patch asked Mike. "Don't get me wrong, but you gotta hear the porch callin'."

Mike smiled. He handed Patch a bowl of pretzels. Pretzels and chips were the only food products that Mike had on hand, and even then, he did not stock much. Any real food he kept would spoil long before it was sold.

"Soon," Mike said. "I still have a few good years left in me. Maybe one day I'll sell this place and buy a boat."

"Where would you travel?"

"It wouldn't be for travel. I'd live on it, just off the coast of Louisiana. That's where I was born," Mike lied again.

The bell on the door rang as it opened, and while Mike kept his smile, his right hand moved beneath the bar toward an automatic rifle that was mounted in a special slot. His index finger felt the contour of the emergency button.

A warm breeze blew in from the outside and two people entered: the guy and girl who worked for downstairs. Mike looked at the small monitor on his computer and squinted his eyes. For the first time since he first met her, the girl had shown up on the detector. He smiled. The new system was working better already.

"That's a nice piece of work, there," Patch noticed as he followed Mike's glance to Freya. "What I wouldn't give to be that age again."

"I was stupid at that age," Mike said.

"She a bit young to be in here?" Patch whispered.

"I sometimes let the local kids 'use the bathroom' if you know what I mean," Mike leaned over as if confiding. "Besides, you don't buy enough to keep me in business. Some days, it's the only thing I sell."

Patch smiled, understanding. "I get it. And they won't buy as long as I'm here. Gotcha, Mike. I'll see you tomorrow. How much do I owe you?"

"We'll settle up tomorrow, Patch. And I appreciate your...understanding that this doesn't get out, capiche?"

"Gotcha Mike. You have a good one."

"I always try," Mike said, waving goodbye.

As soon as Patch left, Mike leaned down as if he were organizing the shelves beneath him. He was actually monitoring both Stone and Freya as they traveled downstairs. He watched as they stepped off the elevator and out of Mike's range.

"They're your problem now, Cole," Mike said aloud as he began closing for the night.

When he got home, he was going to look up boat prices online.

CHAPTER ELEVEN

Stone and Freya entered Ben's office and sat at the two chairs in front of the President's desk. Ben held up a finger before filing some paperwork and turned up to look at them, giving them a professional smile. Ben had been contacted by his boss, Harold W. Smith, who warned him about the various negotiation techniques used by the Masters of Sinanju. But though he was mindful of what was being said, part of Ben was excited. This was a rare historical ceremony that usually only involved kings and pharaohs.

"So, are we ready?" Ben asked, smiling.

"Chairs are not a place to discuss things of great value," Freya started, motioning to the Presidential rug in the center of the office.

"Of course," Ben said, grabbing a thick notepad from the edge of his desk. He sat at the center point of the rug, crossed his legs and looked at Stone and Freya expectantly.

Stone had not counted on Ben understanding the negotiations, much less being excited about them. He lowered his head and muttered to himself. He was going to have to read Ung poetry after all.

Freya sat to Stone's side, but Ben noticed an awkwardness in her movements that he had never seen before. While she was normally moved as gracefully as smoke, she bent over like a normal teenager and even caught her body with her arm as she sat down.

And now that he thought about it, he had heard her steps earlier when she entered his office. Ben's smile disappeared.

Stone took out a few pieces of paper he had folded in his pocket and sat cross-legged next to Freya. He looked at the top page for a moment and then shook his head, as if he were deciding whether or not to continue.

"Is everything alright?" Ben asked. "I understand these negotiations can take some time."

Stone looked up, and Ben could tell that he was embarrassed.

"The Tribe of Sinanju warmly greets the Great American...Chieftain," Stone said. "May history smile on these negotiations."

"Chieftain, eh? Nice. Formal greetings to the Tribe of Sinanju," Ben replied. "Uh, what do I call you?"

"Stone," Stone replied after a moment and then turned back to his notes. "Uh, I'm missing the front page. Freya?"

Freya turned toward Ben and continued from memory.

"The Tribe wishes to thank you for your most kind, generous and benevolent offer of service," she said. "Should these negotiations provide beneficial for both parties, you may feel safe that your throne is protected by the awesome hands of Sinanju. Many generations of your people will benefit from your decision."

"I cannot speak for the United States, of course, only for myself, but I welcome the Tribe of Sinanju. Where do we begin?"

"In our land, it is customary for an exchange of culture and understandings," Freya said. "Throughout history, Sinanju has only been paid in one currency: gold. Before we continue, this must first be agreed: the gold provided will be the purest that your country can manufacture."

"Of course," Ben said. "On what currency exchange do we base its value?"

"By itself. Paper money means nothing to the Tribe. But, if our services please you, it is customary to provide…trinkets as a means of gratuity."

"Trinkets?" Ben asked. The terms of payment were a very delicate discussion topic for Sinanju.

"In the past, Masters who have pleased their contractors, have provided things ranging from jade, to diamonds to the finest silk and rubies. Great rulers have given much to the man who shapes the destiny of their kingdom."

"Noted," Ben said, writing on his notepad.

"Now, perhaps you can share a bit of your culture," Freya suggested. "Something we may not know."

"Well, Stone was born here, so there won't be much he would not know," Ben said. "Freya, America is a nation, young by the five-thousand-year standard of Sinanju, but I believe it to be a great nation. I was not born here, but chose to live here. You will find many cultures within our borders, most working toward the same goal."

"Found it!" Stone said, pulling a piece of paper from another one of his pockets.

Ben turned his attention to Stone.

"A timeless standard of Korean culture is the presentation of Ung poetry. First devised by an ancient master of Sinanju, Ung poetry shares the beauty of a Master's vision with other, lesser peoples."

Ben's jaw clenched. *Here we go*, he thought.

"It is morning," Stone said, trying to keep his food down. "And all is calm…"

* * *

Two hours later, Freya leaned forward to relieve pain in her lower back. She looked around as Stone re-read the part about the bee discovering the flower. She understood the need for such tactics, but Ben seemed to be weathering better than Stone.

Ben, seeing her stretch slightly, used it as an excuse.

"Pardon me for a moment, Stone," he said, interrupting the critical point of the bee finally landing on the flower. "Freya, are you alright?"

Thank God, Stone thought. His center had barely lasted seventy minutes and he was beginning to hate the sound of his own voice.

"I will be fine," she said, but Ben could tell she was hurting.

"I can tell you don't like this any more than I do. How about we move this back to the desk?"

"Sunny Joe expects us to..."

"I've been told," Ben said, returning to his desk. "Spend hours wearing me down to get what you want. How about just asking?"

Stone and Freya returned to their seats in front of the desk. Stone glanced at Freya and then handed Ben the sheet of paper that he and Sunny Joe had privately worked out. Ben barely glanced at it.

"Done. And yes, to Sunny Joe's point, the pay raise will be retroactive to the date you both started working here. Anything else?"

Stone tilted his head in amazement. Obviously, he and Sunny Joe had greatly undervalued their position. For a moment, Stone actually considered bickering with Ben over their price, but there was no way he was going back to the rug and spouting poetry.

"Now that you mention it, there is one thing," Stone said. "Instead of giving me a tip of ivory or crap like that, I want you to use your fancy computers to find my biological mother. And spare me all the arguments about violating privacy laws."

"That is what you want for gratuity?" Ben asked. "That's all?"

"Yeah," Stone said.

"Done. I will need a sample of your DNA as well as everything you know about her."

"I know zilch," Stone admitted. "Except that she was female and a one-night stand."

"That will certainly add to the challenge. Freya? I have no idea what a Mistress of Sinanju would want."

"I had not thought about it, but normally Masters of Sinanju are tipped with jewels or silk or..." Freya tilted her head down in thought. "I know. I would like monthly shipments of wild brown basmati rice!"

"Easy. Please, next time save us all the trouble of the poetry and let's just work this out."

"I will work up detailed notes for grandfather," Freya said. "We will send you the parchment version of the agreement to sign in a couple of weeks. Until then, we have a word bond."

"Agreed. Now, there is something I need and this is not negotiable," Ben said. "I need you to start keeping me in the loop. And telling me the truth."

"Got it, boss," Stone said.

"I wasn't talking to you," Ben said, quickly throwing a pen at Freya. The pen startled her and struck her in the chest. "I actually heard you walk into this office. Compared to how you normally float into a room, you're moving like you have arthritis. Mike was even able to see you on sensors."

Freya bit her bottom lip. "While I still have increased strength and speed, I am not one hundred percent."

"And you expect me to just send a sixteen-year-old girl who

can't even dodge a pen into the field?"

"Mr. Ben, I am not just a sixteen-year-old girl," Freya said, crushing the steel arm of her chair.

"I get it, Freya, you're strong — probably stronger than anyone I've ever known in my life. But you have to realize that you have almost died when you *were* able to center. How can I be expected to send you into the field?"

"You can give me one of your bulletproof armor pieces," she said. "Perhaps a helmet. Whatever it takes for you to be confident in my abilities."

"I can get you a bulletproof vest, but you can't walk around in public with a helmet. You'll attract too much attention."

"I will let Stone lead," Freya said. "And I will only become involved at his direct request."

"Stone, are you okay with that?"

Stone took a look at Freya. He knew her limitations, but he would not embarrass her by making her stay at base or return home.

"She will be fine," he merely said.

"Good," Ben said. "Then let's get back to work. I need both of you in Galveston. There is a small terrorist operation there that might be the tip of a much larger iceberg."

"Galveston?" Freya asked.

"It's in Texas," Stone replied. "What's the job?"

"Take them out," Ben said, looking at his monitor. "But see if you can find out who these guys work for."

"I think we can arrange for them to meet their seventy-two virgins," Stone said.

"Virgins?" Freya asked.

"Uh, I'll explain on the way," Stone said, suddenly realizing that there actually *were* worse topics of conversation than Ung poetry.

CHAPTER TWELVE

Marcus took a long glance at the French Quarter as his chauffeured car passed through. Though Nauru was his nation of birth, New Orleans had been as close to home as anything he had ever known. But, after this week, he would no longer have the simple luxury of a place to call home. If everything worked the way he had planned, and he knew that it certainly would, then he soon would become public enemy number one. The full weight of the United States government would fall upon him. Fortunately for Marcus, the United States government was nowhere nearly as strong or competent as it had once been. Marcus's life would change, but he would survive.

The only wildcard was whether or not Sinanju would become involved. Marcus hated wildcards. While his actions had wide-reaching consequences in the past, Marcus had gone out of his way to keep a low profile, taking great care not to do anything that would necessitate the involvement of the Master of Sinanju. Marcus had only survived as long as he had due to extensive planning and knowing what his enemies would most likely do, something unavailable when dealing with a Master of Sinanju.

Among those who knew such things, it had long been reported

that the Master of Sinanju and his protégé had been hired some time ago by America. It was only with their help that America had continued limping along the last few decades. What was strange was that the Master of Sinanju, an ancient Korean, had been seen many times in the past with his pupil—a white man. When Marcus first heard the news, he discounted it as inaccurate. A Master of Sinanju never took a pupil outside of his own village, but report after report confirmed that this American was performing feats only possible by Sinanju training.

Marcus took a long sip of Tulsi tea and let the moment sear into his memory. In his chosen life of isolation, Marcus had managed to hold on to only a handful of luxuries, so when he was forced to abandon one, it was a major sacrifice.

His car stopped in front of an old brownstone. The house was built almost two centuries earlier by an eccentric old man who was intent on spending every penny he had amassed over his long life to protect him from the outside world. Most people would have thought that such a place would have become a tourist site, but New Orleans was a city where the ancient and the new existed simultaneously. Marcus preferred the sturdy build of stately older houses to the sleek modern lines of contemporary design. To the casual guest, the house was a two-story architectural oddity with marble stairs and polished wood moldings lining the edge of the ceilings. The only windows in the house were in the front living room and the guest rooms.

Even Charles and Ida, the elderly couple that had maintained the house for the past four decades, did not know the extent of the house's secrets. When Marcus took over the mansion, neither questioned him. Their former employer mandated as strict a level of secrecy as the man who first built the house and they were paid well for their silence.

If asked what they knew of the house, they would say honestly that it had six bedrooms, two kitchens and four full bathrooms, not counting the study, den, billiards room and the door at the end of the upstairs hallway. They did not know that the house boasted six other rooms, three secret passages, and two concrete-and-steel safe rooms. The door at the end of the upstairs hallway was merely a front, behind which, if you managed to pry it open, was a reinforced concrete wall. It was never designed to be opened.

* * *

Marcus checked the camera logs on his cell phone one last time. Motion sensors had not detected anything out of the ordinary. Marcus tipped the driver and exited the car.

Entering his home, Marcus headed straight toward his den. He locked the door and sat down beside his desk.

Charles and Ida had been made aware of his arrival on the drive over and were preparing a meal. Neither knew Marcus's true identity or occupation, but they appreciated the light workload and good paycheck.

Though they had served the house faithfully for over fifteen years, and in fact were the closest thing to family that he could claim, Marcus did not trust them any more than he did a random panhandler on the corner. Trust was, after all, a luxury of the masses.

Having given strict instructions never to enter his office, even to clean it, Marcus was relieved to see that the office was exactly as he had left it. The pen he balanced on the edge of the chair near the door was still three-fourths the way leaning away from the door. The soft powdery dust by the doorway had not been disturbed.

Marcus set his laptop on his desk. He punched his intercom button without even looking at it.

"Yes, Mr. Fiorini?" a decidedly ancient voice answered, addressing Marcus by his alias.

"Charles," Marcus said. "I will need you to have my golfing clothes ready."

"At once, Mr. Fiorini. Will there be anything else?"

"Please notify me when dinner is ready," Marcus said and punched the intercom button again.

He looked around and sighed. He was going to miss this place. The New Orleans mansion had been his first American safe house. Marcus had been establishing his network of contacts and made someone's hit list. Little thought was given to taking

Marcus out, so an elderly Italian spy was sent. It took all of six hours to identify and locate the man before he even had a chance to attack Marcus.

Dennis Fiorini, an accomplished spy from the Vietnam era, was far too old to still be in the field. He had retired once, but the allure and money of his glory years was too much to keep him at home.

In the spy community, there is a gentlemen's agreement not to touch a retired spy after a certain age. Fiorini flaunted the unspoken agreement several times. A piece still on the board was a legitimate target, regardless of age. Marcus assumed that he secretly had a death wish, one that Marcus was happy to grant.

Fiorini had known his time was coming. He asked Marcus to not harm his employees and to grant him a swift death. Marcus allowed him a respectful end, and, posing as Fiorini's nephew, took over his properties. Fiorini owned four houses in New Orleans and eight other properties scattered throughout the United States. Marcus investigated each property, but kept only two: the house in New Orleans and a safe house in San Diego. He sold the rest, and scattered the funds across several offshore accounts.

Marcus pulled the flash drive he had taken from Jasir out of his pocket and inserted it into his laptop. He had no idea how a small-time terrorist had possession of something this powerful, but it was obvious that the notes Jasir made were taken directly from the information on the flash drive.

A small window popped up on his laptop screen and a map of

the United States appeared, overlaid with a web of lines, detailing the power grid structure for the entire nation. The words POTUS ONLY flashed impotently at the top. Marcus zoomed the map to Washington, D.C. and paused. His fingers danced just above the buttons of his mouse.

His lesson to America would not be a fatal one, but it would be strong enough to let them know to back off. He moved the map south until it rested over Virginia Beach, Virginia, home to several colleges, three military bases, and a vast number of retirees and tourists. It was a large enough target to make a serious impact, and close enough to D.C. for the government to understand the threat he posed.

Marcus isolated the power grid that provided power for the half million people of Virginia Beach. When he logged into a backdoor to view the computer controlling the electrical grid, he was confused. Instead of the grid layout, he saw a screen from a game called *Planet Warmaker*. Marcus smiled. Whoever was playing games on company time was about to be in for the shock of his life. With a few typed commands, Marcus deprived Virginia Beach of power.

Marcus left the den. Charles was nearly ready with dinner.

CHAPTER THIRTEEN

Ben Cole had finalized his paperwork for the day and entered the dorm room set up for Secret Service agents. The first room housed four wooden bunk beds surrounded by closets, with utilitarian metal shelving on every wall. A small area, which served as a combination kitchen/living area, existed between the dorm area and the bathroom. Ben spent most of his spare time on the couch reading.

Very few amenities were in Ben's living area: a large flat-panel television, a Blu-ray player, and a few movies, but the thing he enjoyed most was the bookshelf that covered an entire wall. Though Ben was never 'off the clock,' he tried to take time to wind down, and nothing cleared his mind better than a good book.

The books ranged from complex studies on Middle Eastern policies to adventure novels about a young boy who was heir to Samson's powers. While Ben did not often read fiction, he did allow himself a few adventure novels every now and then. With his miniature six-hundred-book library, it would be a long time before he would have to scout the local bookstore around the corner.

Ben finished reading and placed the bookmark in his latest novel to prepare for a shower when the alarms began blaring. He raced back to his desk and scoured through the alerts. At first, he could not believe what he was seeing. Every power station feeding Virginia Beach had just shut down. There was no report of explosions or overloads in the system. It was as if someone had just turned the switch off for Virginia Beach.

Ben silenced the alarms coming in from all over the east coast of Virginia and tried accessing the electrical grid's network to determine the cause, but the computers were not responding. Was this a terrorist hack? Though he was unable to access the systems that were down, he was able to make contact with those that were still live. Using that as a map, he traced the effect of the power outage. Everything from the coast to the tip of North Bay was down. Oceana Air Base had already switched to emergency power and was on high alert.

Punching a few keys in panic, Ben breathed a sigh of relief when he saw that the outage came just shy of affecting the Norfolk airport. There were going to be enough casualties as it was without having to compensate for an entire airport.

Ben turned his coffee pot back on and grabbed his cup. It was going to be a long night.

* * *

The technical division of Dominion Virginia Powers Virginia Beach office was located in a small building two miles from the generator. Dominion Virginia Power provided electricity for everything east of Norfolk. The server part of the building consisted of a large, refrigerated room for the twenty-year-old servers, a restroom, and a modest office, barely large enough for the small conference table in the center of the room.

Matt Bowes sat at the table, eating a large sandwich. He had worked at DVP for twenty-six years, climbing the ranks of the once large tech department just before everyone in his branch was laid off.

Everyone that is, but Matt Bowes.

Computers had become so powerful and so smart that the number of people required to run the grid had been reduced over the years. DVP had offered Matt a hefty retirement bonus in an effort to keep three other people with lower wages, but Matt's union contract protected his seniority and all of his friends and co-workers were laid off the Thursday before Christmas.

When Matt complained that he did not have enough of a staff to run the office, DVP authorized an intern from one of the local colleges each semester. In turn for their free services, Matt promised to show them the ropes of his job.

Matt's entire eight-hour day consisted of four simple system checks, each taking ten minutes. He explained to each of the interns that the checks had to be separated by hours so the results would be more accurate. When the interns asked what else he did during his shift, Matt would wink and tell them that he had to keep some things to himself. After ensuring that the interns could run the checks and log them properly, Matt devoted his work time to more important things. In less than a week, he was able to level his main *Planet Warmaker* character to maximum rank.

* * *

Nathan Davis was the latest intern to work at DVP. A sophomore working on an advanced programming degree, Nathan was full of energy and ideas. He had even begun to develop new routines that could help strengthen the decade-old security, but Matt had ignored him. Nathan was not a fool. He knew what was really going on. The sounds of battle coming from his headphones were enough for anyone to know what he was really doing.

Once Nathan found out Matt's *Planet Warmaker* nickname, he made it his personal goal to beat him in online battles every chance he could. Nathan admitted to himself that it was a compelling argument for someone without any chance of a greater future. If he had less drive—if he was like Matt—Nathan could easily stretch one hour of work over eight hours and justify it to people who did not understand technology. But he had greater goals than manning the Virginia Beach electrical grid. Despite Matt's scorn, he had continued to build on his security programming and planned on implementing it during the next server revamp.

Then he saw the warning.

The system had identified unknown credentials accessing the mainframe. Nathan tried to trace the signal, but it rapidly spawned into so many branches that his aged computer could not identify them all. Nathan gave up hope of tracing the signal and began monitoring the system. The hacker had easily bypassed their antiquated server, but the only thing that the hacker seemed to have done was to deposit a small file in their network.

"Hey, Matt, you need to see this!" Nathan said.

The middle-aged man on the other side of the desk sat his sub sandwich down carefully. The last time the new kid tried to get him to look at something, most of the lettuce fell off of his sandwich. To Matt, there were few things more frustrating than having to reassemble a sandwich. That was what he paid the restaurant workers to do.

"What is it this time?" he asked, annoyed.

"I don't know. I think your security was breached, but all I found was just one little file. Hmmm."

Nathan looked at the file. It was a small program, but the hacker had not installed it or even tried to run it.

"Just delete it, kid and reconfigure the security the way I taught you."

"I don't know," Nathan said. "I've never seen anything like this."

Matt sat back in his seat and carefully grabbed his sandwich.

All of the toppings remained inside.

"Kid, when you've been at this as long as me, you see everything. Delete it."

Nathan typed in the delete command, but instead of disappearing, the monitor went dark. Nathan tapped the power button to the monitor, but it was already on. When the screen began working again, it filled with binary code, far too fast to read.

"Matt, you better look at this!" Nathan said, jumping back.

"Dammit, kid, would you let me eat my…"

Matt looked at his screen just as the *Planet Warmaker* scene was replaced by an electronic waterfall. He dropped his sandwich on the floor and began to type.

"I'm locked out!" he screamed, racing around the desk. The code had been run on the intern's computer, so he would only be able to stop the program from there.

"Move! Move! Move!" he yelled, pushing the kid out of the way.

Matt began typing. At one time, when he had first got the job as technical lead for the power company, he was just like the intern, full of energy and ideas. One of those ideas was a personal override that was implanted in the server code. When all else failed, he could enter his code and immediately take control of the entire system.

What Matt was seeing was something he had never thought

possible. Every power grid in Virginia Beach was shutting down.

In his haste, Matt punched in the wrong code the first time and began cursing and slamming the keyboard. Nathan came to his side, ready to learn from the master when the screen went dark once again.

"Uh-oh," Matt said and the lights went out.

"What happened?" Nathan asked.

"Someone just pulled the plug on Virginia Beach," Matt said. He knew he should have retired last year.

* * *

The seven men had met at the same bar every month for the past twelve years. Retired men who had worked for the military, the government, or in politics, they always met once a month to talk about the sad state of world affairs, the glory days, and how they would fix things if they were still in charge. Originally there were twenty-two members of the RSOB's, but their numbers dwindled each year.

"What is that supposed to mean?" the retired director of the CIA asked the white-haired man beside him.

"You know exactly what W. B. means," a former Secretary of Defense replied. "You're just afraid to admit it!"

"I said that you're always griping about your health," the white-haired man said, finishing his vodka and lime. "And if you have a stroke the next time we golf, you're still not getting a bigger handicap!"

"You old bastard!" the former CIA director yelled. "If you weren't so old, I'd show you what a third-degree black belt can do!"

"You've already given us the third degree," someone else chimed in. "It's what makes you so charming."

The former CIA director laughed, leaned back, and downed his scotch. The rest of the men laughed, and then there was a friendly, comforting silence. It was getting late, and despite the personal snipes, the men had grown to respect each other over the years. They had even begun to like each other, though few of them would ever admit it. They were at an age where their families had gone on their own. Their wives had either left them or died, so the members of the RSOB's were the only regular human contact they had.

The weekly meeting had already covered politics, religion, sex, sports, alcohol, and cigars and was winding down into its normal argumentative finale. But before the obligatory 'Go to Hells' could begin, the lights went out.

"Well, damn!" the former Secretary of Defense said. "You guys must pay your light bill like my ex-wife!"

* * *

Sentara Hospital's night shift was always busy, especially on Friday. It was as if the majority of all accidents and emergencies for the week waited until Friday. Extra staff was scheduled, and more doctors were on call, though EMT's and nurses handled the majority of the cases.

When the lights went out across Virginia Beach and emergency power came on at the beginning of the Friday night shift, workers were not too concerned. The power had gone out in the past, but never stayed out for more than a few minutes. It was usually because of something going on at one of the nearby naval bases. Besides, the hospital had priority when it came to restoring electricity, and their generators could power every light bulb in the entire building for hours before they needed to be recharged.

The staff began to worry when an hour had passed and the power had not yet been restored. Dr. Jack Martin was the on-call doctor for the evening. He took a moment off the floor to make a personal call to a Virginia Beach councilman he knew from college. The phone rang several times before it was answered.

"Yes, Jack, what is it?" the man asked, with a long yawn. Councilman Jackson fumbled for his glasses. For some reason, he could not turn his lamp on.

"Henry, the power to the hospital has not yet been restored. We have less than an hour of electricity left in our generators."

"The power's out? I'm sure they're working on it," Henry's sleepy voice said.

"It's never taken them this long to restore power!"

"You have to give them some time on these things," Henry

said. "It's a complicated system."

"Did you even hear me?" Dr. Martin asked. "People's lives are at stake!"

"Have you called Emergency Services?"

"Of course! Everyone is out of the office except for the operator. She said that someone has hacked all of the city computers! Electricity, water, it's all down!"

"Jack, I don't know the first thing about computers..."

"Henry, get your fat ass out of bed and call someone!" Dr. Martin yelled, slamming the phone down.

Useless politician! He lowered his head for just a second before speaking to the nurses around him.

"Everyone, listen carefully. I need you to stabilize as many people as you can and kill every light we don't need," he said. "We're going to lose power within the hour."

CHAPTER FOURTEEN

"You sure you're up for this?" Stone asked.

"I'm paid the same as you are," Freya replied, fidgeting in her seat. "Though I do not like this bulletproof vest."

"Until you can dodge bullets again, it's your new uniform," Stone said. "You'll get used to it."

"The collar bothers me. I cannot turn my head freely."

"Hey, it protects your neck. Besides, you were the one wanting to wear a helmet and that's the next best thing," Stone said. "Heads up, we're almost there. I'm taking lead. You cover my six."

Stone looked at her uniform. Freya had chosen a dark and loose-fitting jacket and slate black gypsy pants. The brightest thing she wore was the dark maroon head wrap that kept her long hair secured to her head. He had come to understand why she kept it—it reminded her of the strange symbiotic bond between her and a sworn enemy who had become her friend, but he never understood why she did not wash off the bloodstains. Freya had refused to discuss it.

"The building we're taking was abandoned years ago. The people we're looking for move from place to place, so it's important we get all of them."

"Understood."

"In situations like this one, I'd feel much better if you'd just let me train you how to handle a firearm."

"I don't like guns," Freya said, pulling several large metal ball bearings from her pouch. "I brought these."

"Ball bearings?" Stone asked, rolling his eyes.

"I have played with marbles all of my life and I am far more accurate with these than you are with your guns."

"Wonder what grandpa would say about marbles," Stone mused. Sunny Joe had berated him several times for using guns and knives.

"He does not know that I am using them," Freya said with a slight twinge of guilt.

"Don't worry. I won't rat you out."

Stone pulled the car over, six blocks from their destination. He lowered his head in frustration for just a moment and then turned to her.

"Sis, once we get to the site, I will treat you professionally, just as I promised grandpa. But right now, I'm your big brother. You're not a hundred percent. Are you *sure* you're up for this?"

"I have access to a few Sinanju tricks and I am still strong and fast. I can do this!"

"I believe you. That's the only reason I agreed to let you come. You're still gonna let me lead and cover the rear."

"I understand," Freya said.

Stone was surprised that she let it drop. The two exited the car and clung to the shadows as they moved to their target. Since Stone could center and Freya could not, it appeared as if she was walking alone. Stone stayed a few steps ahead of her, occasionally scaling the wall to get a better look at the target, an old apartment building that had been condemned so long ago that no one had actually bothered to tear it down. The fire escapes had long ago been torn off the sides of the buildings and the windows had been boarded up.

"I think I can scale the wall and still carry you. It's only six stories, but I lose stealth if I do," Stone said. "You want to wait here while I check inside?"

"You are the leader," Freya said without a hint of sarcasm in her voice. "I will watch the front entrance."

Stone smiled and raced toward the wall. At the last possible instant, he turned his momentum upward and his body clung to the brick and mortar as he passed the second floor, then the third floor—but his momentum began to slow as he reached the fourth floor. Frustrated as he felt gravity reassert its control over his body, Stone turned around to face the ground. Centered as he was, he began to fall in what seemed to be slow motion. As he passed the second floor, he could hear voices. As he reached the ground, his body collapsed in order as he had been taught: right foot, right ankle, left foot, left ankle, right knee, left knee. As Stone bent his hips, he twisted on his back to dispel more kinetic energy, rolling to a stop.

"It is not about sheer speed," Freya reminded him and then lowered her head. "Sorry."

"No, I deserved that. I know better," Stone said. The truth was that he hated climbing walls correctly, because it made his insides feel queasy. It was as if gravity was changed inside of his body and the outside merely reacted to the change. Stone walked to the wall and placed one hand on it and concentrated. He looked up and it appeared as if his body simply started falling upward. He disappeared after passing the second floor.

I need to work more on stealth, Freya thought admiringly. While uncentered, she was unable to spot Stone.

As she turned around to survey the location, she spotted a man on the next block staring at her. Freya moved further into the shadows, but the man continued staring. At this distance, she could only discern that it was a bald man wearing a tan robe. Freya frowned. *There was something familiar about him...*

"Coast is clear," Stone whispered above her.

Freya was startled, but did not make a noise.

"What's wrong?" Stone asked.

"There's a man watching us," she said, nodding down the block where the man had been standing.

But when Stone looked, no one was there.

"Boogeyman, eh?" Stone winked, and then grabbed Freya by

the hand. "Let's go."

"I am serious," Freya whispered, but the man was already gone.

Stone carried Freya up the wall to the roof of the building.

"Roof entrance was locked until I twisted the handle off. I took a peek inside. Top floor is clear, but something is definitely happening on the second floor."

Freya motioned for him to continue. She walked directly behind him. As she did so, she envied the silent glide with which he moved. Her audible steps seemed like someone scraping a chalkboard in comparison.

I will be glad when I can once again center, she caught herself thinking. *Maybe I can center for a few minutes.*

Freya took a sip of air and forced it into the bottom of her lungs. Her ribs separated to allow the breath, but she immediately felt as if knives were slicing through her lungs. She began coughing and leaned against the wall for support. Stone turned around and pulled Freya into a side room.

"What happened?" Stone whispered furiously. "We gotta keep quiet or…"

Stone turned his head. Below him he could hear the stomping of boots and rifles being bolted.

"Damn it! They heard us," he said, moving Freya toward the back of the room. "They're heading our way. Stay here."

Freya started to protest, but remained still as Stone exited the room as silent as a shadow. She pulled at the neck of her bulletproof vest. It was itchy and greatly limited her range of motion. As Stone took his place toward the stairwell door, Freya slid off the offending vest and zipped her jacket high so Stone could not tell she was no longer wearing it. The vest was preventing her from moving naturally, and she needed every advantage she could get. She would have time to explain later.

Freya leaned against the doorway, waiting for the men to open the door. She did not have to wait long. The stairwell door bust open and the staccato explosions of machine gun fire filled the hallway. Freya bit her bottom lip. Stone's body could automatically dodge single fire pistols, but he had never faced a machine gun. After a few seconds of silence, Freya peeked her head out directly in front of a pistol.

* * *

Stone heard the sounds of boots scuffing stairs. If he had counted correctly, there appeared to be at least four men. The stairwell door was to his side. Just before they reached the door, Stone made stomping sounds with his boots. He hoped that it would sound like someone running away.

The door burst open toward Stone and four men lined themselves against the hallway as a fifth man crouched and filled the hallway with machine gun fire. He hoped Freya had stayed inside as he instructed.

Stone re-established his center. He was going to need it.

The man with the machine gun remained crouching and made a forward motion with his fingers. The others went down the hallway, two men to each side, pistols at the ready. The two furthest men passed the room where Freya was hidden.

Stone pushed on the door so hard that it bent back toward the crouching man, almost chopping his body in half. Without hesitating, Stone slid behind the man closest to him. The man barely had time to turn as Stone grabbed his head by the chin and pushed backwards. The leaden snap of his spine echoed down the hallway.

The man furthest to the back turned at the sound and aimed his pistol at Stone, but just before he could fire, something blocked his line of fire.

It was Freya.

And Stone was too far away to stop him from pulling the trigger.

* * *

Freya peeked her head out and immediately felt a presence behind her. Unable to center, she would have to rely on sheer physical force. The man was startled to see a young girl appear in front of him and tilted his gun back just a few degrees.

That was all Freya needed.

She grabbed the wrist holding the gun and twisted up, tearing his hand from his arm. The man shrieked loudly and dropped to the ground holding his stub. His eyes were still closed in pain when Freya kicked him in the chest. But without the control of her Sinanju center, her foot collapsed through the man's back and both fell backwards.

Stone pushed the body of the dead man toward the last of the gunmen, who spent his bullets on the body of his ally. Stone tossed the body back with enough force that both bodies sailed past Freya, who was still trying to pull her foot out of the man's chest.

Stone rolled his eyes as he passed his sister. The last man pulled another pistol and aimed directly at Stone.

Then he pulled the trigger.

Stone had enough time to smile before the bullets reached him. He was not at a level of Sinanju to actively dodge bullets, but his body was trained enough that his subconscious mind could dodge for him. Stone's body involuntarily swung one way and then another. Each bullet passed came within inches of him, but Stone felt no fear.

When the man finished his clip, he reached for another, but Stone was already there. He slapped the gun out of the man's hand so hard that his entire arm went numb. The man squealed as Stone grabbed his good arm and twisted.

"Okay, sunshine, you get exactly one chance to tell me who gave you all of these toys."

"No hablo! No hablo!" the man screamed.

"Oh, you were hablo-ing just fine when you and your buddies were talking below."

Stone twisted the man's arm back until tendons began snapping, but the man hid his voice behind his screams.

"Let me try," Freya said.

Stone noticed her right foot was dragging bloody globules behind her and he immediately caught himself thinking how sloppy Sunny Joe would have thought it was.

Freya leaned into the man's face and told him in her most sincere Spanish that he was going to tell them what they needed to know.

"Vas a decirnos lo que tenemos que saber o el dolor continuará," she said.

The man looked into Freya's eyes, confused. *Was this really happening?* A young American girl giving him orders in Spanish? A man dodging bullets?

The man's thoughts blurred into one searing image as Freya reached behind his back. She was not centered, but she had retained all the knowledge she needed to manipulate the man's nerves through his spine. Her fingernails pierced shirt and flesh and the man screamed.

Without her Sinanju centered level of control, she was unable to control the nerves with any sort of precision. The man went through episodes of explosive diarrhea and heart palpitations as his body's nerves turned off and on. After she finally held her fingers still, the man could not feel anything other than his face. The rest of his body was on fire.

"We are...only a front unit!" he screamed as the pain diminished to a breathable level. "Our leader is on a ship in Galveston Bay called 'Biden's Wisdom'! We are to meet there in two days to get a dirty bomb! I swear! That is all I know!"

"What's your leader's name?" Stone asked.

"Freddy," the man explained and Freya released him to the floor. His heart began spasming out of control. The man took one last breath and then his body collapsed.

"Good," Stone said. "Saves me the trouble. Let's go."

CHAPTER FIFTEEN

Marcus stacked his papers evenly and placed them in a large yellow binder. Another sacrifice made, and yet another luxury gone. The papers were an arrangement that he had drawn up a decade earlier, knowing that this day would eventually come. There were two versions of the papers: one if Marcus was declared legally dead, and the other if he decided to abandon the house in New Orleans.

The first version was kept at a local lawyer's office. It deeded the mansion and the trust fund that financed the property to Charles and Ida Reynolds, the couple who had spent the better part of their lives maintaining it. The other version simply assigned the trust fund to the Reynolds. It would still be enough to keep them comfortable for the remainder of their lives.

* * *

When he had first moved in, Marcus had introduced himself as the original owner's nephew, and presented the couple with a letter of reference. The letter, purporting to be from Marcus's uncle, said that he had needed to return to Italy immediately, and thanked the couple for their years of service. The letter said that he understood if the couple wished to leave, but asked them to consider remaining with his nephew Marcus. The couple agreed to stay.

Charles and Ida had always been professional and respectful, but they were warm, friendly people by nature. Always dodging their questions — *When are you going to get married and fill this big house with children?* — Marcus asked about their families instead. The small details — a granddaughter's wedding, the death of a distant cousin — were a comfort to Marcus, as well as a reminder of a life he would never have.

He found them where they always seemed to be while off-duty: sitting in the small room behind the kitchen.

Marcus knocked on the open door and Charles stood to greet him. He was a very thin man with a face full of wrinkles in all the right places, signs of a full and happy life.

"Master Marcus, it is good to see you, sir," Charles said with a welcoming smile. "Please, join us."

Ida looked up from her cup of mint tea with an equally friendly face. Marcus sat in a comfortable chair beside them, but leaned forward, looking very sad.

"I am afraid that I come with bad news," Marcus said as pleasantly as he could. "Uncle Dennis has passed away and the family has decided to sell the house. I am very sorry, but I have been informed that lawyers will be taking over the property first thing in the morning."

"I am so sorry, Master Marcus. Dennis was such a good man," Ida said, placing her hand over her mouth. "Are you alright?"

"My uncle was a very important part of my life," Marcus lied. "He will be sorely missed."

"It has been such a nice home," Ida said. "But such things do not last forever. Master Marcus, we have been honored to serve your family line."

"As it was an honor to have you," Marcus said. "My apologies for the urgency, but I have arranged for a hotel until you find lodgings elsewhere. Your belongings will be sent wherever you would like them. As per my uncle's contract with you, his estate has maintained a trust fund for your personal care. You will find it to be most generous."

"We cannot stay one last night?" Ida asked, a slight hint of disappointment on her face.

"I am sorry, but I am afraid not," Marcus said. "The lawyers will be here bright and early in the morning. Between you and me, it would not shock me if they were waiting outside right now glancing at their watches."

Charles stood, holding a cup of tea before him in toast. "To Dennis Fiorini!" he said. "May God prepare his way in the world to come!"

Marcus and Ida both stood. Marcus tilted his head forward, acknowledging the toast.

"To Uncle Dennis," Marcus said.

The three sat back down and Ida leaned back on the couch and looked around one last time.

"How long before we have to leave?" she asked.

"A few hours at most," Marcus said.

"Then let us talk of old times before we end things," she said.

They spoke for almost two hours before the limo arrived. Marcus helped them pack a few things. Ida insisted on a hug. As he watched them drive off, Marcus squinted.

Something was in his eye.

CHAPTER SIXTEEN

"Who names a ship *Biden's Wisdom?*" Stone asked as he aimed the small canoe toward the Gulf of Mexico.

Stone's phone vibrated with a text from Ben Cole providing a map of where the yacht was docked, as well as photos. The boat was a vast luxury yacht that had never been sailed since its creation four years ago. Stone and Freya looked carefully at the pictures, quickly memorizing the floor plan.

"He must be a very wise man indeed to have such a grand vessel named after him," Freya said.

"If it's the same one I'm thinking about, the guy couldn't find his shoelaces if they were tied around his fingers," Stone said. "It's gotta be some kind of inside joke."

Cole assured Stone that the Vice President was not on board. He had sold the ship years ago.

"Crap, it's real," Stone said. "Okay, maybe if we're lucky we'll get to sink the boat before we leave."

Freya sat in the back of the canoe, lost in thought.

"Stone, I need to tell you something."

"Can it wait?" Stone asked. "We're on a job."

"It's about the job. I abandoned the bulletproof vest that Mr.

Ben gave me."

Stone looked closely and though she was wearing the same jacket, he could tell that her torso was less bulky than it had been. He should have noticed it earlier.

"Why? You promised that you would wear it!"

"That is why I am telling you now. I am very sorry, but the vest was constricting my movements and slowing me down. I should have said something earlier."

"Dead is a lot slower," Stone said, clearly frustrated. "Fine. When we're through here, we're going back to get it and you're going to wear it. If you don't, I'm sending you home."

Freya lowered her head. "I meant no disrespect."

Stone held his finger to his lips and nodded forward with his head.

The ship in front of them was even larger than it appeared in the photos. Stone guessed that it was easily over a hundred feet long. Though the hull appeared to be made of wood, a closer inspection revealed custom-textured fiberglass. Stone smiled as he moved the canoe to the side of the yacht until he was face to face with the name.

A few quick and silent scratches with his fingernail removed some of the paint from the ship's garish red, white, and blue capital lettering, rechristening it *BIDEN   ISDUM*.

Freya followed Stone as he silently climbed on board. The sole guard on deck was taking a nap on a chair propped up behind one of the lifeboats. Stone tapped the man's temple, insuring that he would never have to bother waking up again. Stone motioned for Freya to follow him. As they entered one of the staterooms below, Stone looked around. It looked like a small hotel room, complete with a television and small refrigerator. The bed in the middle of the room was unmade and Stone, seeing an ashtray, tried unsuccessfully to ignore the scent. He had meant to center himself before boarding the ship. He took a deep breath, fighting back the urge for a cigarette. His breathing partially dulled the nicotine ache that filled his lungs. Expanding his focus to his surroundings, Stone quickly detected the man standing quietly behind them.

The man had seen Stone and Freya sneak in, and had frozen when they entered the room. Normally he would have shot the intruders on sight, but he had left his rifle upstairs when he went to the bathroom. Looking around for anything to attack the intruders, he picked up a pen and slowly approached the man from behind. After he stabbed the man in the neck, the woman would be easy. The man watched Stone bend over to breathe as if he were exhausted from running. He smiled as he raised the pen high over his head.

In one violently swift movement, Freya turned and grabbed him by the collarbone, lifting him off the floor. The man instantly dropped the pen and grabbed her arm with both hands, trying to ease the weight of his body from her grasp. It did not work.

"Where is your boss?" Freya asked.

The man felt his collarbone crack. He tried to scream, but something about her grip also silenced his vocal cords. He looked down at the devil girl holding him with one hand, not knowing what to do. He could neither scream nor answer her question. So when she let him back down, all he wanted to do was scream the answer so the pain would not return.

"The bridge!"

Stone grabbed the man by the back of the neck and twisted. The sound of dominoes falling echoed in the room as his vertebrae snapped one after the other.

"Thanks, Freya. I've still got lead, though," Stone said.

"I understand."

Stone left the cabin and seemed to float across the deck. Freya followed, hugging the shadows where she could. They approached the front of the yacht and Stone made a motion toward a door. Freya saw the door flash open for a split second, and then Stone disappeared inside. Before she could reach the door, Freya heard several crashes, the last of which was the result of a man being hurled through the bridge window. His broken body landed in Galveston Bay.

Then the bridge filled with gunfire.

Freya broke through the door, crashing into a man firing a pistol. The bridge room was almost forty feet long, spanning two floors. Stone was toward the helm at the front. Four men stood at the back firing at him from behind a table, but each shot missed. Centered or not, Freya knew that Stone could not continue to dodge this many bullets in the open for long.

She dove into the midst of the men firing from the back, sliding razor-sharp fingernails deep into their backs. Their hearts began beating erratically and then stopped. One of the men tried to fire his pistol one last time, but his shot went wild, striking the ceiling. Freya slapped at the back of his throat and moved to the next man, who was aiming at Stone from the corner. She grabbed his hand and squeezed until the metal seemed to merge with flesh and bone. His scream was loud enough to get the attention of the men in the middle of the room.

Seeing Freya at the back and Stone at the front, two of the men in the center of the room began firing at Freya. She ducked behind the table at the back and was pinned down by bullets. One of the men decided to target the table itself and Freya felt the impact of each bullet as it chipped away at the expensive oak.

Stone had finished the last of the men in front when Freya entered. Her sudden and loud appearance had startled him to the point that one of the bullets ripped through the sleeve of his shirt.

He returned his concentration on surviving, but there were too many men in too many places. Stone dodged behind the wheel and looked over to assess Freya's situation. She was trapped in the back.

* * *

Freya felt the first bullet tear through the table four inches in front of her face. She crawled behind the body of one of the men who had fallen behind the table, but when she entered, the men had seen that she did not have a gun. It would not be long before one of the men simply ran back to her position.

"*Offense!*" she heard Sunny Joe yell in her mind. "*You can't win unless you're on offense!*"

Seeing that Stone was occupied up front, one of the men reloaded his pistol and ran toward the table. Freya saw him from behind the dead man she was using as a shield, but before he could fire, his head disappeared from his body.

Stone had ripped the wheel from its floor mount in the helm and hurled it at him. The wooden steering wheel tore through the air too fast to be seen. The man never knew what hit him.

Freya peeked from behind the table. She never saw the gunman who approached her from behind.

But Stone did.

The moment froze as he weighed his options. He dropped to the floor and hurled himself past the men who were firing on him, taking two of them out as he passed. Stone focused on the gunman who was aiming at Freya. There was no way he could reach Freya or the gunman in time.

As if in slow motion, Stone saw the gunman lift his rifle to his shoulder and pull the trigger. The bullet spiraled towards Freya's head. Stone knew that while she was uncentered, she could not move out of the way quickly enough.

She was going to die unless Stone could stop the bullet from reaching its grim and inevitable destination.

Stone leapt directly into the bullet's path, hoping that his bulletproof vest would take the hit. His body began to twist out of the way, but Stone concentrated. At first, his body hesitated and he twisted back, but Stone willed himself into the path of the bullet. He had often compared the feeling of dodging bullets to riding a roller coaster. His body took control and he was bounced one way and then another in whatever direction needed to avoid the bullets—but now it felt as if he had been hurled off the roller coaster and into a wall.

The bullet caught the inside of his left arm an inch from his own bulletproof vest. Stone felt the intense heat of the bullet as seared and tore through his skin. He could feel it inside of him, and there was no escape. The bullet struck an artery and Stone instantly lost control of his body.

He crashed hard against the wall, and he did not get up.

CHAPTER SEVENTEEN

From a nighttime satellite's perspective, Virginia Beach did not exist. The once brightly-lit city was now pitch black, as everything from traffic lights to water pumps had stopped over the past few hours. Emergency teams had tried their best to restore power, but the grid itself had not been damaged. The controls had all been computerized years ago, and until the computer system was either repaired or replaced, no one in Virginia Beach was going to see a single watt of electricity.

Looting patterns changed once people realized that the electronics they were stealing were useless without power. They began to target grocery stores more than electronic shops. Police stood in busy intersections directing traffic with flashlights. The Salvation Army had donated several generators to local hospitals. Churches and synagogues had opened their doors to the needy. The community as a whole was coming together.

But they were still in the dark.

Ben tapped into ground crew communications, trying to get a grasp of what was happening on the ground, but, as he feared, the system itself was not broken. It had just been turned off, with no way of turning it on again. The electrical grid had become so dependent on computers that it would take a replacement of the entire network and a re-haul of the entire grid.

That would take several months and millions of dollars and Virginia Beach did not have that much time.

One of Ben's monitors was dedicated to coverage of the blackout. Reporters from all over the country had descended on "The Dark City" to cover the mayhem.

To keep the short attention span of their viewers, one of the networks set up a crawl at the bottom of the screen to keep a running tally of injuries and deaths. Injuries were reported in a blue box at the bottom left of the screen. It made a swooping sound and glowed every time another injury was reported, while deaths were tallied in a red box at the bottom right. It made a deep thumping sound and shook each time the number of deaths increased.

So far, injuries outnumbered deaths 34 to 5, but the anchor assured his viewers that if they continued watching, he was certain that the numbers would go up.

CHAPTER EIGHTEEN

Finally seeing the gunman behind her, Freya retreated toward the cover of the table. She saw Stone moving towards her, but knew that even at Sinanju speed he could not reach her in time. Freya saw Stone's body twist as it unconsciously attempted to dodge the bullet, but, instead of moving out of the way, Stone's body moved directly into the path of the bullet. Unable to do anything more than watch the bullet strike her brother, something in Freya snapped.

Instead of moving for cover, she found herself moving toward Stone. Once he was down, he would be helpless against the gunman.

Freya was not about to let that happen.

She leapt over Stone as he hit the wall. The gunman was already drawing a bead on Stone. Her arms flailed wildly, distracting the gunman. He started to aim his gun at her again and even pulled the trigger, but the bullet passed by harmlessly.

Freya landed in front of the man and without thinking, grabbed him by the head. She hurled him toward the last two gunmen, snapping his neck. The sight of his soaring body caused the men to raise their hands in defense. Freya jumped in front of the men. Without the precision of her Sinanju center, the blows were bursts of brute force. She began at the shoulders, relieving the men of their weapons. The follow up punches splintered ribcages and pulverized hip bones before the instantly-dead gunmen even had time to fall.

The loosely-connected bags of meat plopped to the floor and Freya ran back to Stone.

"Two more…around the corner," Stone said, handing Freya his gun.

Freya pushed the gun back into Stone's hands and pulled a couple of steel bearings from her pocket.

She slowly approached the corner, listening for any signs of life. Her un-centered hearing was not good enough to tell what was around the corner. Fortunately for her, Stone's was.

"They're hiding behind something. I can hear them wheezing," Stone said, bringing himself to a sitting position. He grabbed his shoulder. "Careful, sis. We need one of them alive if possible."

Freya readied one of the bearings in each hand. From her vantage point, she could see several boxes readied for shipping. The men must be behind one of the boxes. Freya looked around at the scaffolding in the ceiling and then to the far side of the room.

* * *

Fasil and Jaleel hid behind separate shipping containers, both holding grenades in their hands.

"The American fights like a demon," Fasil said. "He dodges

our bullets as if they were stones. Let us see if he can dodge shrapnel."

"Shush, Fasil! I think Muhammad killed him," Jaleel said. "The gunfire has stopped."

"Then why has Muhammad not returned?" Fasil asked, surprised that his stupid cousin was chosen to be a part of the glorious branch of the family that would topple America.

Fasil heard a sharp click and turned to see Jaleel laying down, taking a nap. Jaleel was as stupid as his mother. He had no idea why his uncle married her. But Jaleel was not sleeping. Fasil noticed the pool of blood seeping from Jaleel's back and looked all around. He had not heard a gun, not even a silencer, which were not as quiet as American movies made them appear to be.

Jaleel pulled the pin on his grenade. If they took him out, he would take them all with him.

When he heard the next sound, he looked down to see a small object embedded into the back of his forearm. It was not a bullet, though it was metal. The object had struck so fast that his body had not yet recognized the pain. What he did recognize after seeing the object in his arm was that it had caused his hand to involuntarily open.

Fasil tried to throw the grenade away, but his fingers were still stuck, so he began flailing his arm to shake the grenade off his fingers. He succeeded just before the grenade detonated, giving him time to partially hide from the explosion. The grenade shredded his left shoulder and shrapnel embedded into his ribs. Fasil staggered behind another crate, coughing blood. A thin, blonde-haired girl appeared in front of him.

After expecting camouflaged soldiers, she seemed surreal. *Was he dead? Was this the first of his seventy-two virgins?*

"Who are you?" he asked.

"My name is Freya," she said. "And I need some information."

"Don't take another step!" Fasil yelled.

"I don't think you want to die," Freya said. "I just need you to answer a few questions and we will leave you in peace."

Fasil could not believe what he was hearing or seeing. "Where are the soldiers who killed my brethren?" he demanded.

"Oh, it's just the two of us," a voice said from behind, grabbing Fasil by the back of his shirt.

Fasil turned to see a tall American holding him. Blood stained the left side of his shirt, but he did not act as if he were hurt. Fasil screamed, but Stone grabbed him by the face and twisted. The shock to Fasil's spine was enough to drop him to the floor. The pain continued as the American continued talking.

"I'm not going to ask nicely," he began. "Your friend shot me, and I'm not too happy about that."

Stone closed his eyes for a second and grabbed a breath. Freya raced to his side. Stone motioned for her to stay back. He had to show strength.

"You get one chance, and only one chance, to answer my questions," Stone said.

Fasil watched the American carefully. His boastful words tried to cover the extent of his wounds, but Fasil knew it would be a matter of time before he fell.

"I want to know about your…network," Stone said, searching for the right words to say. "Sleeper cells."

"I will tell you everything you wish to know, Infidel," Fasil said, smiling. He would take his time with long, bloated answers, leaving him with only the girl to contend with. Even wounded by a grenade, he could easily take out a skinny American girl.

"Our network consists of four families. We have lived in this wicked country for years beneath your very noses! We follow the lead of the Ghost Imam."

Stone blinked twice. The words were blending together. He began coughing, but could not regain his center.

Fasil smiled even more.

Stone rubbed his eyes when Fasil made his move. Fasil leapt, punching Stone in the stomach long enough for him to grab a detonator from the counter.

"You will now die!" Fasil said, pressing the button.

But the signal from his brain never reached his thumb. In fact, it never reached his hand, because Freya was now holding his severed hand, detonator and all.

Freya's calm face became a storm. Fasil tried to run, but she shattered his shins with a swift kick. His body went into shock. He tried to walk, but his legs only twitched in response.

"I think it is time that you saw your virgins," Freya said, grabbing Fasil by the back of his shirt. She dragged him to the edge of the ship and tossed him over. The seawater burnt his exposed wounds like acid. Fasil tried to swim, but with only one working arm, he only remained afloat for a few seconds.

Freya scooped up Stone in her arms and carried him back to their boat. She lowered him down with one hand as she crawled down. As soon as he hit the boat, Stone collapsed. Freya began furiously paddling the canoe with one hand and dialed Ben on her cell phone with the other. He did not have time to say hello.

"Stone has been shot!" Freya said. "I cannot stop the bleeding!"

Ben took a quick moment to locate Freya and stabbed a few quick buttons on his keyboard.

"Listen very carefully, Freya. This is what you're going to do," he said.

CHAPTER NINETEEN

Paul Moore had never been Sunny Joe's friend, but he never relished conflict with him. He had seen Sunny Joe's father physically deal with an uncooperative council, and was thankful that Sunny Joe listened to the council at least some of the time. Still, Paul had run across him too many times not to feel the presence that all Masters projected when they were angry.

The first time he felt it was from Sunny Joe's father, Joseph Roam. The former head of the council had actually yelled at him in public. Joseph did not yell back, he merely lowered his head and even though Paul was not the target of the gaze, something made him feel small, like a child. The only thing keeping him from running was the knowledge that running would not save him. Joseph merely took one step toward the head of the council and placed one finger in the center of his chest. The council leader dropped to the floor, unconscious, and Joseph demanded a recount of votes.

The formerly unanimous vote instantly switched to Joseph's side.

Paul had never wanted to be the leader of the council, but once he was appointed, he did not run from his duties. The problem, Paul realized, was that the Sinanju tribe was shrinking. Tribal deaths outpaced births two-to-one, and they were constantly losing their young people to the big cities that offered plentiful jobs. Paul knew that unless something changed, the time would soon come when he would have to do the unthinkable and try to remove Sunny Joe from office. He did not know if the council had such power, but if *something* was not done, and done quickly, it would no longer matter. There would no longer be a Sinanju tribe to defend.

Paul entered Sunny Joe's office and he gave a cautious smile and nod to Dale, who was sitting behind the counter. Dale was a realist like Paul, but his friendship with Sunny Joe had blinded him to Sunny Joe's deficiencies.

"They finished setting up for the ceremony?" Dale asked.

"It's taken most of the day just to clean up the council chamber. First time in memory they swept and mopped the floor. Old Man Jenkins even washed the stained glass window," Paul said, referring to the only piece of stained glass on the reservation: a four foot tall window on the back wall that had been purchased by the Arizona government in an early effort to add 'culture' to the building. Located on the western side of the building, it cast an eerie blue, green and gold swatch of light over the rest of the chamber late in the day.

"Leroy actually working? That's something monumental enough for me to record," Dale joked.

"Need to speak with Sunny Joe," Paul said.

Dale finished typing the sentence he was on before giving his full attention to Paul. "I just hope it's good news," Dale said, motioning Paul to go back.

"Dunno if Sunny Joe will think so, but it's good news for the tribe," Paul said.

Dale followed Paul as he knocked on Sunny Joe's door. Sometimes being the tribal records keeper was not a fun job. He knew of the tension between Paul and Sunny Joe and recognized the look on his face.

"Come in, Paul," Sunny Joe said, recognizing the heartbeat on the other side of the door.

Paul opened the door and sat in one of the chairs in front of Sunny Joe's desk. Dale silently sat in the other and turned on his tape recorder. Sunny Joe smiled and nodded at Dale, then his face lost any pretense of kindness as he faced Paul.

"What is it this time, Paul?" Sunny Joe asked, staring a hole through him.

Paul was just as tall as Sunny Joe with a stronger frame. Normally, he would not be intimidated, but height or strength meant nothing to Sinanju.

"It's about the Coushatta boy," Paul said. "The council is going to give him sanctuary. By the end of the day, he will be Sinanju."

Sunny Joe leaned forward. "And you didn't think it would be

worth asking me?" he asked.

"We already know where you stand, Sunny Joe," Paul said. "And even though you disagree with the council, we expect you to abide by our decision."

Dale concentrated on writing down what he was hearing, ignoring the awkward silence.

"The boy is lying," Sunny Joe said.

"You've said that, but unless he is somehow a threat to the tribe, I don't see how that affects our decision. What is he lying about?"

"Why not ask him?" Sunny Joe said. "You can't estimate a threat if you're not aware of it."

"This isn't about Sinanju business," Paul said coldly. "If the boy becomes a threat, I assume you can handle him."

Sunny Joe returned Paul's glare. "The council can make whatever decision it wants. I'm just telling you that something's not right with his story. Have you contacted the Coushatta?"

"They will only say that the boy's parents died in a car wreck a few years back and that the boy left of his own free will last year."

"That suspicious story doesn't bother you at all, Paul?"

"No, it doesn't. But do you know what does bother me, Sunny Joe? The Sinanju. We were a small tribe to start with, and we're shrinking more every year. You know how many kids stayed at the reservation after they graduated last year? Two!"

"The senior class only had four graduates," Sunny Joe pointed out.

"It's a simple game of numbers, Sunny Joe, and you can't dodge or attack the fact that if we keep going down this path, in forty years, there won't be a Sinanju tribe!"

"That's what my pop was saying forty years ago, Paul."

"And our tribe was twice the size then as it is now. Sunny Joe, we need new blood."

"That's what it's always been with your line, Paul, hasn't it? It's always about blood."

Paul sat back at Sunny Joe's dig. Paul was a direct descendant of the original ruling line of the Sinanju, before Kojong arrived.

Savage warriors had attacked the tribe. Kojong defeated them, but not before the Chief and his two sons were killed. Normally, the lineage would fall to any bastard children of the chief, but the people chose Kojong to lead their people over the chief's bastard son.

The descendants of the original royal line attempted a coup some time later. All of the participating families were forever banished from the Sinanju. Paul was a descendant of the only royal member who did not attack. What Sunny Joe did not realize, nor anyone except for Paul and his late mother, was that Paul was also the son of Sunny Joe's father. His mother had forbidden him from ever mentioning it, telling Paul that it would mean an immediate exile from the tribe.

At his mother's funeral, Paul almost told Sunny Joe. But he had made a promise.

He clenched his teeth before speaking again. "If this was about blood, Sunny Joe, you would know it," Paul said.

"That a threat, Paul? Just 'cause I don't handle the council the way my father did doesn't mean I'm going to let you push me around."

"I'm not gonna give you cause to remove me from office, Sunny Joe," Paul said. "But the sad fact is that our tribe is dying, and our chief doesn't give a damn."

Sunny Joe leaned forward.

"Dale, please note that I did not remove the head of the tribal council leader," Sunny Joe said, motioning for them to leave.

Dale grabbed his pad of paper and followed Paul out of Sunny Joe's office.

"I can assume you're still going to be at the ceremony, Dale?" Paul asked.

"It's part of the job," Dale said. "Listen, Paul, you know I agree with you on this. We need to do something, but I've learned to trust Sunny Joe on these things. If he says something is wrong, then it's worth checking out."

"No offense, Dale, but you're his friend. It's hard to take advice from someone who is biased."

"No offense taken. But really, my friendship with him aside, I'm giving you my honest opinion."

Paul leaned over the counter. "Sunny Joe is treating you for your sickness, Dale and you guys have been friends since childhood. C'mon, you gotta admit that doesn't exactly make you unbiased."

"Nor does it make me stupid. You have your say, Sunny Joe has his. I can see both sides."

"Dale, the man is never going to see our side. Let Sunny Joe know that he has a formal invitation as well as his traditional seat at the front."

Paul walked out and shut the door. He knew that Dale would be there to record the event, but he hoped Sunny Joe would just stay away for once.

* * *

Tekoa's swearing-in ceremony was held at the council center late in the afternoon. It had taken most of the day to prepare for the ceremony. The front tables had been folded shut and stored in the back and the place had been thoroughly cleaned top to bottom. Folding chairs were assembled into a circle at the center of the room. One chair and a small table were set in the middle of the circle.

People began showing up around four, but even with the council, Dale and a few of Tekoa's friends, it was a small ceremony.

Sunny Joe showed up at the last instant, but chose to sit at the back of the room where Dale was recording the event instead of the chair set aside for him at the front of the circle.

Other than Sunny Joe, everyone in attendance was excited. This was the first time someone had been initiated into the Sinanju tribe in over three generations.

"You gonna stop this?" Dale asked Sunny Joe.

"Nope," Sunny Joe said. "Just wanted to make my protest noted."

"It's the first thing I wrote down," Dale noted. "I wish you'd reconsider, though."

"For what it's worth, I hope I'm wrong," Sunny Joe said.

* * *

As head of the council, Paul stood before the other councilmen in full ceremonial regalia. His formal headdress was nothing compared to Sunny Joe's tribal crown, but it was still gaudy. Golden threads interlaced each of the four columns of feathers, gathered together into a small knot at the front. A bronze symbol of the Sinanju tribe covered the knot, resting between his eyes. His robe was a flowing maroon, with golden lightning bolts and stars on the front. The other councilmen wore their civilian clothing as most of them had either lost parts of their tribal garb, or it was so moth-eaten that it was unwearable.

"We welcome our brothers and sisters to this solemn ceremony. In a hundred years, no one has been initiated into our tribe, but today, the tribe of Sinanju gains a brother. Tekoa, come forth!"

Tekoa walked from the back room, dressed in his civilian clothes, covered with a deerskin shawl. He walked between the chairs and stood before Paul.

"Behold our new brother Tekoa, who has renounced his ties to the Coushatta. He seeks to walk the path of the Sinanju," Paul said. Then he took a deep breath and glanced back at Sunny Joe. "Are there any present who would deny his claim?"

The entire room simultaneously followed his glance, but Sunny Joe remained perfectly still. After a few seconds, the crowd seemed to exhale simultaneously.

"Then take your seat, Tekoa, as we show what it is to be Sinanju."

Tekoa sat behind the small table in the center of the room. Paul placed a small, clay plate on the table. It was very old and obviously handmade, imperfect in both shape and thickness. In the middle was the symbol of the tribe: a trapezoid, bisected by two lines.

"This represents our tribe," he said. "The whole of everything that binds each one of us together."

Paul pulled a small bag of rice from his pocket and emptied it on the plate into a mound. He moved the rice with his fingers until the symbol in the middle of the plate was visible.

"Rice represents life; our daily toils, harvests, the dust and the rain, our laughter and tears, births and deaths."

Paul placed an ancient small coffer in front of Tekoa. A thin band of gleaming gold decorated the edges of the box, but the wood had been darkened by age. The symbol of the Sinanju tribe was carved on the lid. Paul opened the coffer and brought out four tattered feathers, which still boasted a bit of their original bright blue hue. He placed them tenderly at the top of the plate.

"These were taken from the headdress of our great father Kojong, who traveled across the great western sea. It is he who saved our tribe in the dark days, when others sought to eradicate the Sinanju from the face of the Earth."

It was a small reaction, but Sunny Joe noticed that Tekoa flinched when he heard Kojong's name. It might have been something as innocent as the boy being fidgety, but the timing was curious.

Paul placed the last of the tokens on the plate: a large, smooth stone.

"Kojong brought this stone from his home village, across the great sea. It represents the Sunny Joe, blood descendant of Kojong, to whom we all swear allegiance," Paul said, glancing back at Sunny Joe. "He is the center of our life, the defender of our tribe. Without the Master, there is no tribe."

Again, Sunny Joe noticed a slight shudder in Tekoa. He was at least subconsciously disagreeing with what Paul was saying. No one else noticed. Sunny Joe sighed in frustration.

Dale noted the sigh. "What's wrong?"

"I'll tell you later. This is not something that needs to be recorded. Not yet, at least."

Dale went back to detailing the ceremony. Paul had placed soot on his index finger and was tracing the symbol of the Sinanju on Tekoa's face. He started with the trapezoid, drawing it around his eyes.

"The trapezoid represents the centered state of a Sunny Joe. No matter how much larger it is on top, Sinanju remains perfectly balanced."

He drew two sharp lines down Tekoa's face, lining them up with his eyes.

"The strong lines represent power. The House from which we come has one line. We are second and thus, display two lines."

Dale took out a camera and took pictures of Tekoa with his Sinanju war paint. Tekoa tilted his face down a bit, but Paul grabbed his chin and pulled it back up. Dale finished taking pictures and then the final part of the ceremony began. Two cups of hot tea were placed before Paul and Tekoa. The subtle smell of Korean herbs permeated the room.

Paul handed Tekoa his cup of tea and then picked up his own.

"We now drink as brothers. I present you to your new family, the brothers and sisters of the Sinanju."

Both took a drink of the tea. Tekoa winced at the strong taste.

"Are you ready, brother Tekoa, to take on the name of the Sinanju?"

"I am," he replied.

"This day," Paul said. "You devote your life by blood oath to the Sinanju."

Paul removed a knife and grabbed Tekoa's hand. He sliced the back of Tekoa's forearm and Tekoa tried to pull back. Paul moved Tekoa's arm over the mound of rice.

"Two things are demanded of all Sinanju," Paul continued. "You recognize the Sunny Joe as your tribal leader from this day forward. You pledge your honor to the bloodline of Kojong and to follow the precepts of our tribe. Secondly, you pledge not to offend the House of Sinanju from which we all come, in either action or word. Do you agree to these terms?"

"Yes," Tekoa said. "I do."

Paul grabbed Tekoa's forearm with both hands. The other elders of the tribal council circled around Tekoa and placed their hands on his shoulders. They began chanting in a strange language, a blend of the tribe's original language and Korean, the language of Kojong.

Tekoa seemed embarrassed.

After a few minutes, each of the tribal councilmen shook Tekoa's hand and bowed. Paul glanced back to Sunny Joe, but he remained in his seat. He was making it publicly clear that he wanted nothing to do with this decision. After the last of the councilmen were seated, Paul moved to the front of Tekoa and splashed a mixture of white and black powder on his face.

"From Kojong's example, we have welcomed those who have sought sanctuary over the centuries. Tekoa, the blood that flows through your veins is now Sinanju blood. Your brothers are the men of the Sinanju. Your sisters are the women of the Sinanju. You are now authorized to take part in ceremonies, marry, and be buried on Sinanju land."

Paul smiled and shook his hand. Most of the room erupted in cheers.

Sunny Joe left in silence.

Dale continued to write notes, wishing that life had less drama.

CHAPTER TWENTY

Freya sat in the back of the ambulance next to Stone. Her makeshift tourniquet had been replaced by bandages, and Stone's arm was hooked up to an IV. Tears coursed down Freya's cheeks and she cursed herself. If she had not been so selfish about her own comfort, Stone would not have been shot.

"We've got him stabilized," the technician said. "He's gonna be okay."

Freya could tell that the man was not as confident as he sounded. Stone had lost a lot of blood. If she were able to center, Freya could try to put him into temporary hibernation, slowing down his bodily functions to a crawl. She had not yet graduated beyond manipulating the nerves of the spine, but she was aware of the other access points: the wrists, neck, palms, ears and bottom of the feet were all rich in nerves that affected the rest of the body.

She strained her memory for the correct procedure, but was unable to remember. Without an exact guide, she could inadvertently give Stone a stroke. Freya bowed her head and held his hand tightly.

"Please hurry," she whispered.

The technician avoided eye contact, trying to keep from

frowning.

The ambulance pulled into the emergency room and Stone was rushed to the operating room. Freya entered the waiting room and sat down on a worn plastic chair in the back corner. She bowed her head and began praying for forgiveness to the gods of her mother.

"Choices have consequences," she could hear Sunny Joe saying. "And you can't change a consequence. At that point, you can only learn from it." But at the moment, Sunny Joe's wisdom just seemed like a bunch of hollow words. They meant something at one time and perhaps would again, but right now, they meant nothing to her.

* * *

Twenty minutes later, Freya was half-lying on the waiting room couch. She had not heard anything since they took Stone into surgery. She tried to watch television to distract her, but the few programs she scanned made sure that she would watch even fewer programs in the future. She thumbed through the magazines on the coffee table, but the only magazines available were about fashion and fishing. The fashion magazines were filled with bizarre headpieces and half-nude models. She had never seen anyone wear anything like that and wondered who would buy such clothing. The fishing magazines were equally bizarre. It was designed for people who used poles and lures. Freya's mother had taught her as a toddler how to grab fish with your hands and, when she got older, how to skin them with your fingernails. She found the articles about 'reading the minds of bass' to be quite humorous. The author suggested that a fisher could emulate the movement patterns of fish by understanding their needs. If she were not waiting for news about Stone, she would have laughed out loud.

Her cell rang, taking her out of her haze. She left the waiting room when the caller ID displayed 'Colonial Pizza.' That was Ben Cole's code number.

"Hello, Mr. Ben," she greeted. "Stone is still in surgery."

"The surgeon just finished. He said Stone is going to make it," Ben replied. "But he will be taking it slow for a while."

"Thank you, Mr. Ben!" Freya said, her immense relief making her cry again.

"Now that we know he is going to survive, would you mind telling me how a man who can dodge bullets was shot?" Ben asked.

Freya swallowed hard. "It was my fault," she said.

"How is that?"

"After our first stop, I removed my bulletproof vest. During the second fight, one of the men had me in his sights, but instead of dodging out of the way of the bullet and letting me be shot, Stone dodged directly into the bullet."

"I thought he couldn't control his dodge."

"That's what I thought, too. But that's what happened."

"Freya..." Ben said and then the line went silent for a moment. Freya could just see the vein on his forehead sticking out, which happened when he was frustrated. She had only seen him mad once and she had never forgotten his face.

"Freya," he continued, his voice more controlled. "Our safety protocols do not take into account fashion or comfort or anything other than your protection."

"Yes, Mr. Ben."

"We just signed a four-year contract. Is this what I can expect from Sinanju?"

"No, Mr. Ben. It won't happen again."

There was a long pause. It did not take Sinanju hearing to detect the veiled sigh on the other end of the phone.

"Freya, I have never hid the fact that I did not think you should be in the field with Stone, but my boss believes that because you are being trained in Sinanju that you are worthy of field work. The truth is, you're *not*. And you won't be for several years. If you want to live that long, you are going to have to second guess yourself before you second guess others."

"Yes, Mr. Ben."

A nurse walked into the waiting room and Freya all but dropped her phone. She raced to meet the nurse at the door.

"Is he okay?" Freya asked.

"Your brother is out of surgery and asking for you," the nurse said.

"I will call you later, Mr. Ben," Freya said, closing the connection.

The nurse led her to one of the small recovery rooms located behind the operating room. Freya entered the room and smiled as she saw Stone moving. The nurse closed the door behind them.

"Sis?" Stone whispered. "What happened?"

"You're going to be alright. They took out the bullet."

"What does Cole know?"

"Everything. He arranged for a CURE doctor to work on you."

Stone looked around wide-eyed and struggled to sit up.

"Never should have involved him," Stone grimaced, trying to fight the drugs in his system. The doctor was advised that Stone was to have the minimum amount of drugs necessary, but even the low dosage was messing with his system. *Guess my body has already started to change*, Stone thought.

"The doctor saved your life," Freya said. "They said that the bullet struck an artery. You were bleeding out."

Stone leaned close to her. "And if I had started talking through the delirium of the drugs, the doctor also was told to kill me."

"Mr. Ben would not do that!" Freya protested. "Would he?"

"Sis, the contract protects us from Ben, but there are field protocols in place for situations like this, and they have nothing to do with him."

Freya's eyes narrowed in concern.

"We'll talk more about it when we return home," Stone said.

"Mr. Ben said that you would be out of commission for a couple of days."

"Yeah, I'm not laying in a hospital bed for two more days."

"Your body needs time to heal," Freya said.

Stone could hear the concern and the guilt in her voice.

"This wasn't your fault," he said. "I chose to dodge into the bullet."

The floodgates opened and Freya bent over Stone, sobbing.

"I am so sorry!" she said, wiping her runny nose with her sleeve. "I never should have taken off my vest!"

"What does grandpa say about consequences?"

"I don't care," Freya said. "I thought first of my personal comfort and you paid for it!"

"Well, look at it this way: I am a little closer to being able to dodge a bullet now. I didn't know that I could aim myself *into* a bullet."

"Promise me that you'll never do that for me again," Freya said.

"Can't do that, sis. I'm not gonna let you take a bullet intended for me."

Freya grabbed a tissue and began dabbing her eyes.

"I won't let you down again," she said soberly. "I promise!"

"You can't promise that either," Stone said, forcing a half-smile. "I don't care how far along you are in Sinanju, you're still human and that means that you're gonna screw up."

Freya leaned over and softly hugged her brother. For that moment, she was not a Mistress of Sinanju, a member of the Sinanju tribe or even a child of Lakluun. She was a sister.

Stone pushed her back, took a deep breath and found a weak center. Normally, his body would be flooded with superhuman power and expanded senses...but between the surgery and the drugs, he felt barely able to walk.

"Let's find my clothes and get out of here," he said.

CHAPTER TWENTY-ONE

Ben Cole pinched between his eyes. He had been staring at the raw code used to override the electrical grid for over an hour. No matter what he tried, no matter what information was given to his powerful new computers, the answer was always the same: change the parameters of the original program that hacked the grid.

That meant finding the original computer that was used, and that was not going to happen.

Ben leaned back in his chair and closed his eyes. His two agents were deadly, but not experienced enough to be in the field. It would only be a matter of time before one of them ended up in the morgue, and then what would he do? He had been given a field command, but only two troops. He had warned his boss that two agents, regardless of their skill, would simply not be enough. Even when he had seen the amazing things that Stone and Freya could do, his optimism had been dulled by the real-world fact that life in the field often depended more on experience and luck than strength and skill. What were they thinking by putting a sixteen-year-old girl in the field?

It had been an order, not a request, but perhaps Ben should have protested further. And perhaps after this, he could insist on Stone going alone until Freya had more training. But their contract had stipulated an all-or-nothing deal.

His computer lit up and began beeping.

A new trail.

Ben bolted forward in his seat, scouring the information that was scrambling across his monitor. Someone had just logged onto the computer that had hacked Virginia Beach and was scouring the web with a signal. The signal was complex, far more complicated than a home computer. If Ben's computers were not so powerful, it would likely have taken days to decode the signal.

The signal routine traced the signal to New Orleans. After a few seconds, it even showed the house from where the signal was originating.

But why?

The phone rang.

"Where to next, boss?" Stone asked.

"Aren't you supposed to be in the hospital?" Ben asked.

"I got better," Stone said in a mock British accent.

"Why are you talking like Ringo Starr?"

"Sorry, boss. The drugs they gave me are making me...a bit loopy. They'll be out of my system soon."

"I hope so, because someone has knocked Virginia Beach back to the Stone Age."

"A nuke?" Stone asked with a tinge of worry.

"No, thankfully, but they've found a way to cripple all power in the city."

"So what's our assignment?"

"Stone, I don't think you're ready to go back in the field. You just left the hospital—earlier than doctor's orders, mind you—and you just said that you're still drugged."

"Ben, just give me a few hours and I'll be fine. Maybe not a hundred percent, but good enough for government work," Stone said, immediately regretting his choice of words.

"I don't like this one bit, Stone, but this is important stuff. Just promise me that you'll abort immediately if you don't feel that you're up to the task."

"You have my word."

"I've traced the computer that shut down Virginia Beach to New Orleans. You need to be careful. The location just made itself visible, so I'm concerned that it might be an ambush."

"Thanks for the heads-up," Stone said.

"I'm sending you the address now. You have to grab the computer or we could face this situation again."

"Is there a target?" Stone asked. "The guy who owns this computer?"

"If you find someone, take precautions to bring him back alive. We need to find out how he got the initial code. He made it appear to have come directly from the White House. If the President's personal access has been hacked, America's in trouble."

Stone's phone beeped and a small map displayed a New Orleans address.

"Snatch and grab it is," Stone said.

"You'll have a plane waiting for you." Ben paused before continuing. "Are you sure you're up for this?"

"We didn't just sign a four-year contract to quit during the first week," Stone said, hanging up.

Ben punched in a few orders, setting the computer on a deep scan. He needed to find out everything about that house before Stone and Freya arrived.

As he began typing, a window popped up on his screen, responding to an earlier request. It was Stone's DNA report. The lab had rushed the results per Ben's orders, but he had not expected a response so soon. Ben printed the document, shaking his head. That was yet another sign that he was working with amateurs. Ben would have easily paid Stone twice what he had asked for, but their only additional requests were to find Stone's biological mother and for monthly shipments of rice.

Ben returned to tracing the presidential code that had been used to shut down Virginia Beach. The monitor in front of him filled with information concerning the house in question. The owner was listed as Dennis Fiorini, a native of Italy, but in the original documents, his birthday was listed as September 14, 1928. His most recent tax records were listed as September 14, 1968, not quite an understandable mistake.

It only took him ten minutes to find out why. Dennis Fiorini was a known Italian spy who had disappeared some years ago. Ben's blood ran cold when he read the last line of Fiorini's file. He had come out of retirement for one last job: to kill Marcus Eames.

CHAPTER TWENTY-TWO

The sun had just set when Stone and Freya entered the quiet, stately neighborhood in New Orleans. The sounds of the day had already surrendered to the evening life of the French Quarter. Freya was watching how Stone was walking.

"Are you feeling okay?" Freya asked. "You're not centered."

Stone glared at her for a moment before softening his stance. "I'm okay. I'll center once we reach our destination."

"I'm wearing my bulletproof vest this time, see?" Freya said, showing the collar-to-waist armor.

"Just cover the rear," Stone said. "The guy who cut power to Virginia Beach is inside. Cole says take him alive, but if we encounter any resistance, take him out." Stone was dying for a smoke, but some smartass doctor had thrown away his cigarettes while he was unconscious.

Freya noticed the edge to his voice and though she did not say anything, the worried look on her face spoke louder than words.

Stone slowly sipped in a breath and centered. For a moment, he seemed to have disappeared. "Better?" he asked.

Freya nodded quietly. "Any special instructions?" she asked.

"We're going in, grabbing the guy, and taking his computer. Fast," he added. "His computer is more important than he is, so we don't want to damage it."

"What is on his computer?"

"I don't know, but I've never heard of a terrorist who has just one bad idea."

"True," Freya said, adjusting her collar. She agreed to wear the restrictive body armor, but she still did not have to like it.

The pair strolled past the target building, and Stone and Freya pretended to be a couple of friends walking by, laughing and talking. Both stole glances at the house as they could, mentally taking notes.

"He did not say anything about bars on the windows," Freya noted as they stopped a block away.

"Are you sure you don't want a pistol?" Stone asked.

"I may have agreed to wear your restrictive body armor, but I draw the line at having a gun. It takes all of my concentration away from my hands."

"Then you better keep your little steel marbles at the ready. This guy may be dangerous," Stone said, motioning for them to move out.

Stone snuck onto the grounds ahead of Freya and perched on the small roof above the front door. Freya smiled and walked to the front porch as if she were visiting a friend and knocked on the door.

A large man wearing a dark suit opened the door.

* * *

Stone's ex-SEAL buddy Dozer hated wearing suits, but even

after he was cleared for the murder of his commanding officer, none of his Central and South American contacts would have anything to do with him. Dozer had to find work stateside, working with celebrities and visiting dignitaries, and that required wearing a suit. Over the past few years, Dozer had worked his way up the food chain to the point he was getting the occasional mercenary job. In a couple of years, he would be back on track.

Today, however, he was a glorified doorman.

He loved easy jobs like this. Guarding paranoid men was easy money. You dressed nice, acted tough, went home, and grabbed some sleep. Wash, rinse, repeat for a week or two until they realized that they were in no danger. Take the money and on to the next job. Dozer felt nothing for the man he was guarding. Their relationship was merely an agreement of time and money, nothing more.

So when a teenage girl walked up the stairs and knocked on the door, Dozer radioed as he had been instructed to do by the man upstairs.

"Got some kid at the front door," Dozer said.

"Threat level?" Marcus asked.

Dozer scoffed. The girl could not have been eighteen. She was tall and thin, and the way she moved did not indicate any hostility.

"I got this," Dozer said and cut the connection.

The girl looked around as she waited for someone to answer the door.

Dozer smiled. He was about to scare the living daylights out of this little girl. The door busted open and Dozer filled the doorway with his body. He looked down at the girl and scowled.

"Go away," he growled.

"Dozer?" a voice from behind the girl asked.

Freya turned to see Stone standing behind her. "You know this man?" she asked.

"Yeah, he gave me my contacts in Central America," Stone said.

"Winner?" Dozer asked, searching the man's face. "Is that really you?"

"I go by Stone now. Wow, don't you look cute."

"What are you doing here, man?" Dozer asked, obviously irritated. "I'm on a job."

"So am I," Stone said.

An awkward moment of silence passed between the two men until Dozer pulled his Glock and placed it in Stone's face.

"You need to leave before this gets serious, Dozer," Stone said.

"Winner, you saved my life, but we're even," Dozer said, holding the pistol steady.

"My name is Stone now," Stone said. "This is your last chance to leave, Dozer."

"Sorry, man," Dozer said and pulled the trigger.

Unlike people who were unfamiliar with firing a pistol, Dozer never blinked his eyes when pulling a trigger. He waited for visual confirmation that the target was hit.

But something weird happened after Dozer pulled the trigger. Stone's face became blurry for a split-second. After the gun had discharged, Stone's face had been right where it was before. Dozer noticed that Stone, however, was now the one holding the gun, and felt confused. His confusion intensified when the girl picked him up with one hand and charged back into the house with him. Dozer had no idea how she was strong enough to pick him up, but he was about to put her in a world of pain. His foot swung toward the girl's head, but his hip felt as if it had exploded as the girl slapped his leg out of joint.

"If you are one of Stone's friends, stay down," Freya said.

Dozer was sprawled on the wooden floor, blinded by pain. It was as if the girl had somehow torn his leg out of its socket and it was only attached by skin. The girl turned her back to him long enough for Dozer to take a throwing knife out of his pocket.

He threw the knife with all the force he could muster and knew it would strike her square in the back. But something came between the girl and the knife. Stone caught the blade between his fingertips.

"I never said he was a friend," Stone said, hurling the knife back with the force of a rifle.

It embedded into Dozer's forehead so deeply that only the handle showed.

Marcus Eames had been watching the scene unfold from the various cameras in the front parlor. He was safely sealed in the third-floor panic room, and from his concrete and steel-reinforced fortress, he had access to cameras in every room from multiple angles.

He punched the code for the front door and hit rewind. He saw the blonde haired girl knock on the door as Dozer described. Then a man that Marcus had not noticed appeared behind the girl as suddenly as a ghost. Marcus paused the video and zoomed in on the man's face. He was young and about as nondescript as you could get without plastic surgery. Average nose, average jawline, and average brown hair. What was not average was what happened once Dozer placed his pistol in the man's face. The man did not look worried, even when Dozer pulled the trigger. And the man was still standing there after Dozer pulled the trigger.

Sinanju? Marcus caught himself thinking. Everything he had read about them told him no, but he knew of no other method to achieve the movements that the man did without attributing them to Sinanju. But, Marcus reasoned to himself, if this was an apprentice of Sinanju, where was the Master? And who was the girl? If one or both of these people were Sinanju, there were a number of inconsistencies.

The man is obviously in his early twenties, far too young to be the American Sinanju protégé who travels with the elderly

Korean.

He carries a pistol, which is taboo for Sinanju.

The man's wrists are of normal proportion, but his reflexes are fast enough to catch a knife.

Dodged bullets fired at point-blank range. Regardless of inconsistencies, this must be Sinanju.

The girl is the true puzzle. Sinanju never trains women, but she picked up a two-hundred-pound man as if he were a loaf of bread. Girl must be apprentice—or attached to apprentice in some way.

The girl is a wild card.

Marcus cursed his luck. He hated wild cards.

Twice before, Marcus had cheated death by leaving a scene before the Master of Sinanju arrived. Eventually, he knew that his luck would run out—and he also knew that he would have no chance of surviving such an encounter. It took several years of research, but he devised a plan that, if successful, would not only allow him to survive, but would actually protect him from Sinanju indefinitely.

The dangerous part was surviving long enough to implement the plan.

Marcus punched the panic button, but as soon as he heard the sounds of steel doors sliding into place, he felt a crash of thunder that shook the entire house. And then another crash. And another.

Marcus's security system showed that the steel door guarding the stairs no longer existed. Marcus switched his attention to the girl. From what he had seen in the video, the girl was superhumanly strong. Marcus opened one of the panels that linked him to the secret passageways scattered throughout the house. He grabbed a small box and shut the panel behind him.

If this did not work, he would not return.

"They always hide on a higher floor," Freya said, dropping the steel door that had previously protected access to the stairs. "They believe that more layers increases their security."

"Yes, what's it called? 'The Lesson of Layers,'" Stone said, and for a moment, conceded that Sunny Joe's explanation of fortress security was pretty accurate regardless of the actual layout.

Sometimes he hated when Sunny Joe was right.

"I'll take the upstairs," Stone said. "You secure the entrance in case the target decides to bolt. We want him alive, but if he becomes a threat, take him out!"

Freya nodded and returned to the entrance. She was not going to fail Stone a second time. The front door was still closed and the body of Stone's former SEAL teammate remained in the awkward angle where it had landed.

She stood by the entrance, peering through the small window in the middle of the door. Had she been centered, Freya would have detected the slow, shallow breathing in the dark corner of the room behind her. Had she been centered, she would have detected the chemically-soaked sponges hurled at her and she would have dodged them.

But she was not centered.

The sponges hit her in the side of the head, releasing a musky liquid that quickly took her breath away. Freya tried to hold her breath, but the fumes had already seeped inside her nasal passages. Freya turned toward the source of the sponges, but her eyes were already stinging. The world seemed to tilt and Freya spent her last energy trying to wipe the substance from her face before collapsing to the ground, where she lay very still.

Marcus picked her up and slung her over his shoulder.

"Guess she isn't Sinanju," Marcus said to himself, heading back to the secret entrance.

CHAPTER TWENTY-THREE

Stone cautiously glided up the stairs, mindful of any sounds around him. His senses did not detect any motion sensors or other tremors that would indicate a trap. As he reached the second floor, he expected another steel door, but while ornately carved, the door was wood. His senses told him that nothing was beyond it. Stone palmed the door and it fell back on its hinges.

So much for subtlety.

A small hallway led between the open door and another doorway at the end of the hall. As he held himself toward the edge of the hallway, his cell phone began vibrating.

Not now, he thought, but one glance told him that he had to answer.

"Not a good time, boss," Stone whispered.

"Stone, you and Freya need to leave right now."

"We haven't acquired the target yet."

"Abort and regroup."

"Hello," a voice said from speakers hidden in the ceiling. "I have your friend, but don't worry. She is safe. For now."

"Where is she?" Stone asked, ignoring Ben.

"She is my guest. My name is Marcus Eames and I wish to

negotiate an exchange."

"Stone, don't do it!" Ben yelled. "You cannot trust this man!"

"He's got Freya," Stone said.

Ben could hear the anger in his voice. "Stone, I have been exactly where you are right now."

"I doubt that."

Ben slapped his desk hard enough to hurt his wrist. He closed his eyes.

"I know that right now, you are about to disobey my direct orders, so listen to me very carefully: Eames's strength is his intelligence. But there is no way he could have prepared for a Master of Sinanju, even one in training. Determine what skills you have that he cannot account for and when you strike, strike hard."

"He's a dead man," Stone said coldly.

"Stone, no matter what you think, you are not ready for this man," Ben replied and hung up.

Stone closed his eyes and listened. The house had several distinct creaks, but in the background, he heard Eames talking. Stone could not make out what he was saying, but he knew the direction. Stone bolted to the top floor and opened the hallway door. His senses turned him away moments before an explosion ripped through the door, blowing smoke and debris past him. Stone cautiously peeked around the corner.

On the opposite end of the hallway stood Marcus Eames, holding Freya in front of him. The hallway between them was gone and a fire had started below. It would be a matter of minutes before the whole house caught fire.

"You said you go by Stone, right?" Marcus asked.

"Freya!" Stone yelled. Whatever had happened to Freya, she was barely conscious.

"I expected better from a Sinanju trainee," Eames said. "Here is what is going to happen."

"What's going to happen is that I am going to tear your throat from your body," Stone said.

"I have no doubt you could do that, but there is the slight problem of your partner."

Stone looked at Freya, who was doing her best just to remain standing. Marcus held her dangerously close to the railing, and if he let go, she would hurtle into the fiery destruction below them.

"So what's your cause?" Stone asked. "Allergic to peanut butter? Didn't get enough balloons on your eighth birthday?"

"I want to make one thing clear," Marcus said. "I am not declaring war, or attacking Sinanju in any way. I am simply sending a message."

"A lot of people died for your little message," Stone said.

"People die all the time, but you never seem to notice unless they're American. I just exploited a weakness in your system. They died because your defenses weren't good enough. If your country can't handle a little bloody nose, then America needs to just expand that wall you're trying to build and hide from the rest of the planet. Because out here—in the real world—it's not all peanut butter and balloons."

"Thanks for the sermon. Now, you want to give me my partner back? You can give her back now, and then I kill you, or I kill you first. What'll it be?"

"I can see that this girl is important to you. But why?" Marcus paused, edging even closer to the railing before continuing. "If she were male, I would consider her a Sinanju trainee, but she doesn't move like Sinanju. Besides, Sinanju never trains women. Either way, it's...unsafe for her to be out here."

"If you're so concerned, why are you using her as a human shield?"

A smile, almost too brief to see, flashed across Marcus's face. "Because it works. Now, this is what is going to happen," Eames said. "You are going to pledge Sawon Ahm and then I am going to present you with the computer you are looking for as a present. And then I am going to leave."

"Saw what?" Stone asked.

"Sawon Ahm—the Sinanju blood oath."

"So after I pledge Saw-whatever, then what?"

"I present you with my computer, then you go your way and I go mine."

"What about her?"

"That is entirely up to you."

"Let her go and I will say whatever you want me to say."

Marcus leaned Freya over the flames. Her knees began to buckle. Stone leaned forward waving both arms.

"Okay! I pledge by Sow…" he began and Marcus pulled her back.

"Sah…Won…Ahm," Marcus slowly said.

"I pledge Sawon Ahm," Stone carefully repeated.

"A client always presents the Master with a gift for Sawon Ahm. The computer is in the room to my right. I also present you with the girl's life. I don't kill children."

Marcus lowered Freya safely to the floor and Stone crept across the length of the hallway's wall until he was standing face-to-face with Marcus Eames. He made sure to get a good look at the man who made Ben Cole so nervous.

"So much for you being a master strategist," Stone said, leaning in to rip Marcus's head off. But before he could attack, Stone he felt something grab his leg.

It was Freya. She was shaking her head back and forth, trying to clear it.

"Sawon Ahm," she repeated. "It is a sacred vow. This man is now our ally."

"He tried to kill you!" Stone screamed.

"We are each responsible for our actions," Freya said. "You have invoked Sawon Ahm. All of Sinanju is bound in a blood treaty with this man."

"That's bull, and you know it!" Stone shouted.

He leaned in again to strike, but frustration pooled like poison in his veins.

Freya was right.

Stone had allowed himself to be suckered.

"Tell the Master of Sinanju about our deal," Marcus said as he walked toward a room in the back. He turned one more time to face Stone. "And stop bringing innocents into the field. It is unprofessional."

Freya slowly stood to her feet. The fog in her head was still muddling her brain. Stone found the laptop from the room behind them just as Eames had said. He picked up Freya, and, slinging her over his shoulder, climbed out a back window. One door in the house had already exploded, and he did not want to risk the entire house collapsing around them.

"Wait here," Stone said. "I'm going to finish business with Mr. Eames."

"No, Stone! We will not further embarrass Grandfather!"

"What?"

"I have been thinking about what Mr. Ben said. We are embarrassing the tribe to the point that our enemies trick and belittle us. I will not return to the field until I am healed and can once again center. You need to fully heal before returning to duty."

"So we basically tell Cole that we're calling in sick?"

"Recouping from injuries is in our contract," Freya said.

"You actually read the thing?"

"I wrote it," Freya said.

"Then you can explain it to me later," Stone said. He looked at the computer and frowned. No matter what Freya said, he felt cheated.

CHAPTER TWENTY-FOUR

Before returning the Sinanju council chambers to its normal arrangement of seats and tables, the council threw a welcoming party for Tekoa and his friends. They cleared the floor and filled a table with hot dogs and snacks. With few tribal functions, all of the high school's sixteen students had come to the party.

One of Tekoa's friends brought a boom box, filling the chamber with dance music. The council sat around the edge of the room watching the youngsters talking and dancing and laughing. Tekoa looked at them and imagined that they had probably been wallflowers their entire lives. He walked over to Paul Moore and sat next to him.

"Mr. Moore, I really want to thank you for believing in me," Tekoa said. "I won't let you down."

"Ah, someone has to stand up to Sunny Joe every now and then to remind him that he's not a king," his friend Tommy said. "What a joke!"

"Mind that tongue," Paul said. "It's one thing to disagree with Sunny Joe. It's another thing entirely to publicly mock him."

"What's he gonna do?" Tommy asked. "He can't hurt members of the tribe! It's Sinanju law!"

"He can't, but I can," Paul said. "Sunny Joe and I disagree on many things, but you're about to get on my bad side."

"Come on, Tekoa, it's beginning to smell like old people here," Tommy said.

"Thanks again, Mr. Moore. I won't forget what you did for me," Tekoa said. "And, uh, sorry about Tommy."

"That's okay. We were all young and stupid once," Paul said, pointedly looking at Tommy. "Go on, have fun. And again, welcome to the Sinanju."

The party continued for another ten minutes before Tommy started talking about Sunny Joe again.

"So, Sunny Joe just sat in the back with his arms crossed the entire time!" Tommy said. "Like he was gonna stop it or whatever! Useless old man!"

Tekoa laughed so hard that it hurt.

"And then when the ceremony was over, he was gone!" Tommy said. "Like the ninjas he's always making fun of! Sunny Joe can't stop my man Tekoa from becoming Sinanju!"

The friends high-fived and then Tekoa looked at his watch.

"Hey, man, I gotta be at work in the morning, so I'm gonna head out and grab some sleep."

"See you tomorrow night?" Tommy asked.

"If Old Man Jenkins doesn't have me doing his dirty work, I should be off by five."

"You need a ride home?" Tommy asked. He had just qualified for his driver's license and strained for any excuse to drive his dad's station wagon.

"Nah, I like to walk," Tekoa said.

"Cool. See you after supper, then."

"Later," Tekoa said. He grabbed the few presents the council had purchased for him—four sets of new work clothes and a few used CDs.

Tekoa walked the quarter mile to the Motel Sinanju. It was late enough for the air to be cold, but the night was peaceful and the sky was clear. Without all the light pollution of the city, he could clearly see the Milky Way.

This is how it should always be, Tekoa thought. *How it was meant to be.*

Tekoa reached his motel room and saw another small package by his door. He fumbled for his key and opened the door. The package was hastily wrapped in butcher paper and tied with twine. A small piece of paper signified that the package was from the motel manager.

Tekoa took the box inside and opened it.

It was a souvenir Sinanju coin from when the Motel was first opened. Designed to look like a Las Vegas token, the tribal image was boldly stamped on both sides with Asian writing etched on the sides. Tekoa took one look at the coin and tossed it into a box near the bed and locked the door. After making sure the blinds were closed, he pulled out his cell phone and manually dialed a number.

"Status?" a voice asked upon answering.

"You were right. They let me in."

"What about Roam?" the voice asked, referring to Sunny Joe's civilian name.

"He knows something's wrong, but he is too weak to stand against the council."

"Good," the voice said. "Then they won't know what hit them. What about the girl?"

"She is more Sinanju than her brother, but I'm working on her," Tekoa said confidently. "She has no friends other than her brother and Sunny Joe."

"Don't you *ever* call him that!" the voice yelled. "His name is Bill Roam and he is *not* the rightful ruler of the Sinanju!"

"Sorry," Tekoa said. His boss was touchy when it came to Sunny Joe.

"Don't forget, Tekoa, the Sinanju stole our power and that power is ours to regain!"

"I said I'm sorry. I'm just trying to blend in."

"You're doing well," the voice said, calming down. "Very well, indeed."

"When do we strike?" Tekoa asked.

"Be patient. Take time to endear yourself to the Sinanju. Help whenever you can. Become a trusted friend. We have waited hundreds of years to get to this point. We can afford to wait a few more months."

CHAPTER TWENTY-FIVE

Ben sat quietly at his desk, looking over the mission notes he had jotted down. He glanced at the earlier mission notes he had on Stone and Freya. The escape of Eames made three failures on their part.

Three strikes.

But Ben's hands were tied. They had just signed a four-year contract. Ben made a mental note that this would most likely be their last contract. The luck they had exhibited so far could not be counted on to continue in the field. Sinanju trainees or not, one or both of them would probably be dead within the year. Freya's inability to center made her an extreme liability in this mission, and Stone was not yet ready for solo missions, either. And his protectiveness of Freya created its own problems.

Stone literally took a bullet for her.

For a moment, Ben about calling Sunny Joe and asking his honest opinion to see if that mattered, but the alarm signaled the bar doors opening above. The new computers automatically tracked the new visitors. It was odd seeing Freya on the camera system. Mike nodded at the two, smiling, no doubt believing that their new security system was allowing her to be tracked. But Ben could not tell him why his sensors and cameras would never pick her up unless she wanted to be detected. It was need-to-know.

Ben placed all of his papers in a small folder as Stone and Freya entered his office. Stone's eyes were almost sealed shut in pain and Freya sat in her chair more meekly and dejected than he had ever seen her.

"How are you doing?" Ben asked Stone.

"Freya and I have been talking. We've been pushing ourselves a bit hard," Stone said.

"What Stone means is that we are invoking section four, clause two," Freya said. "Until we are properly healed, we will not be able to provide the level of service for which you have so graciously paid. Until I can once again center and Stone has recovered from his gunshot wound, we will be unavailable for service."

"How many more times will you go out before one or both of you are killed?" Ben asked. "Two? Three?"

"Stuff it," Stone said, handing the laptop to Ben. "We got your precious computer."

"Only because Eames left it," Ben noted.

He turned the computer on and connected it to one of the new secure lines. It instantly logged in to the program Eames had used to cut power from Virginia Beach. The map showed tiny red dots detailing exactly which stations had been hit. After verifying that his new security had not been breached, Ben let the program contact each of the power stations. The small red dots began to flash and then turn green as the computers returned to their original operations.

Power returned to Virginia Beach.

"The man keeps his word," Ben said. "Too bad that you have to keep yours."

"Hey, I didn't know what San Am or whatever was."

"I do," Ben said, leaning forward. "How can you know less about your own culture than me?"

"I realized what he was doing," Freya said. "But I was too weak to stop him."

"Screw him," Stone said. "The next time we see him, he's dead meat."

"I don't think so," Ben said. "The reputation of the House is the most important thing you possess. If you have sworn a blood oath with this man, it applies to all of Sinanju. You. Freya. Sunny Joe. Remo—your father—and Master Chiun. All of you."

"They don't have to know. Eames is a dead man," Stone said.

"You cannot attack him, Stone," Freya said. "It is forbidden."

"After what he almost did to you?"

"Unless he attacks us first, Mr. Eames is an honored ally of the House and Tribe of Sinanju. He has to make the first move."

"Believe me, someone as smart as Marcus Eames will never do anything that stupid," Ben said. "With one small move, he has just removed the entire House and Tribe of Sinanju from being a threat to him."

"Fine. Sue me," Stone said. "I'm not in the mood right now."

"Then maybe you will be in the mood for this," Ben said, sliding a piece of paper from under the folder in front of him.

"What's that?" Stone asked.

"I found your mother," Ben said.

"That's great news, Stone!" Freya said, smiling for the first time since arriving.

"That was fast," Stone said. He grabbed the paper and read every word. He no longer felt his injury. He no longer felt weary. His hand reached toward his mouth and Freya could have sworn that she saw tears welling up in his eyes.

"Is this real?" Stone asked. "Is this really my...mother?"

"According to your DNA, Rebecca Fitzpatrick is your biological mother."

Stone stared at the paper and the words seemed to blur together. According to the report, his mother was once a nurse, trying to take care of both of her parents. She had no brothers or sisters and no reported children. She ran into trouble in her mid-thirties after her mother died and she had to put her father into a nursing home. She spent eight years in state prison and her nursing license was revoked on six counts of grand larceny. She currently lived in a small house in White Plains, New York, doing paralegal work.

The last paragraph caused Stone's eyes to widen. It listed her address and phone number.

"When can I see her?" Stone asked.

"That's up to you," Ben said. "I'm just fulfilling my part of the bargain. By the way Freya, monthly shipments of wild basmati rice will be sent to your address starting next week."

"Thank you, Mr. Ben," Freya said.

"I'm flying to White Plains tomorrow," Stone said.

"You mean 'we,' right?" Freya asked hopefully.

Stone felt a selfish twinge about seeing his mother for the first time and slightly turned his face away.

"Not this time, sis," he said softly. "I've got to do this on my own."

"Is everything okay?" Freya asked. "What does the paper say?"

"Just let Sunny Joe know what happened. I promise that I'll tell you everything when I get back. Can you trust me on this, sis?"

"Of course," Freya said somberly. "If that is what you want."

"You can stay in the bunk room for the night if you wish," Ben said to Stone. "Freya, your flight to Arizona leaves in four hours. I will call a cab for you."

"Thank you, Mr. Ben," she said numbly.

Ben and Stone left for the barracks, leaving Freya alone in the faux Oval Office.

CHAPTER TWENTY-SIX

The weak bulb from his porch light enabled Dale to see around his bedroom. Lying in bed, he stared at the ceiling and tried quietly to catch his breath. It didn't work, and the pain continued its constant roar near his heart. Dale placed his face into his pillow to cough and when his wife stirred, he gave her a soft kiss and she rolled over. He did not want to awaken or worry her. There was nothing she could do. Sunny Joe had tried to help with his nerve therapy and while it had put off the pain, eventually even his treatments failed to work.

At first, Dale's wife had suggested that the pain was just from his body getting old, but Dale knew otherwise. You and only you *know* when you are in love; you *know* when you are in pain.

And you *know* when you are dying.

She had tried to lift his spirits by exercising with him, and had even changed her diet to a healthy one in order to assist him in his own, but Dale could think of few tortures worse than limiting his remaining meals to kale and rice.

When he was first diagnosed with lung cancer in his early fifties, Dale immediately checked in to a Texas treatment center. After months of therapy, he received a clean bill of health. Dale had quit smoking, he had begun a regular exercise routine, and he began eating healthier. He felt better than he had in decades, and thought his cancer days were over.

Then two years ago, Sunny Joe told him that he smelled cancer on Dale. Dale did not believe him until he began feeling a familiar tingling whenever he had to cough. The tingling morphed into a familiar ache: a thin, slicing pain that seemed to branch through his lungs.

Sunny Joe finally ordered him to see Doc Hodges, and the tests confirmed that his lung cancer had returned.

Dale and his wife took off for a two-month vacation, leaving their eldest son Victor in charge of records, but all Dale could think about were the mistakes he was going to have to correct when he returned. In desperation, he had done the unthinkable by asking Sunny Joe for help. He should never have put his friend in that position.

But what else could he do?

Doc Hodges had recommended that Dale should return to the cancer center that had treated him the first time, but the treatment had been torturous and he swore that he would never go through that again. Doc Hodges tried to reassure him that technology had advanced a great deal in the last two decades, but Dale did not want to take a chance and end up a vegetable like so many of the others he had seen.

It was his life, and he wanted to die on the Sinanju soil where he would be buried.

The stack of papers sitting on the small desk on the other side of the bedroom was testimony that he was behind on his work. He was so far behind that he did not even want to think about his assignments next month. His wife had suggested that he let Victor take over for a while so he could rest, but Dale knew what happened to his father and his grandfather after they stopped working—they died.

Dale stared at the top dresser drawer. Inside was the gun his father had bought Dale for his twelfth birthday. He never needed it for safety. Crime was non-existent on Sinanju land. He had used it a few times for target practice, though. Once, Sunny Joe even let him do his best to try and shoot him. After Sunny Joe's reassurance that he would be okay, Dale blindfolded him and told him to turn around. Sunny Joe was not only able to dodge every bullet that came his way, he was able to catch them as they passed and drop them neatly into a pile at his feet.

That was the first and only time that Dale felt fear around Sunny Joe. He knew that Sunny Joe was a Master of Sinanju, but knowing and seeing are two very different things.

If Sunny Joe could not cure him, he had no hope. He could only look forward to several months of pain and nausea until it was too much for him to handle, until his body finally stopped.

There was a quick way out, though. Sunny Joe's father had taken it when he found out that his mistress had died. All it took was a single moment of clarity. One bullet. One quick pull of a trigger and it would all be over...

Dale looked over at his wife as she lay sleeping peacefully next to him. A soft smile stretched across her face. Dale shoved the thought back down into the dark recesses of his mind where it belonged.

CHAPTER TWENTY-SEVEN

Sunny Joe sat next to Freya on the small outcropping of rock behind her house. She was sitting with her arms wrapped around her legs, her body language so tight that she was denying access to her own feelings. She had been quiet since returning from their mission alone. Sunny Joe had a hard time getting her to talk about it.

"Mr. Ben found Stone's mother," Freya finally said.

"Is he sure he found the right woman?" Sunny Joe asked.

"The D and A test was a perfect match."

"DNA," Sunny Joe corrected. "Though don't ask me what it stands for. I just call it 'white magic' like my pop did."

"Mr. Ben gave Stone a paper telling him where she lived, and he just left," Freya said.

"Did he say anything else?" Sunny Joe asked.

"Just to tell you that he would be back after he has spoken with his mother," Freya said. "I hope it goes well."

Sunny Joe put his arm around Freya. Even though he was close to Freya, it was Stone who made her feel part of the family.

"So," Sunny Joe said, trying to change the mood. "Tell me how the client looked when Stone started reading the Ung poem."

Freya involuntarily grinned despite herself. "Mr. Ben's boss had some experience with Sinanju negotiations through Master Chiun, so I thought he was prepared, but after the first two hours, he interrupted to ask about me."

"Never allow a client to interrupt. To obtain a satisfactory result, we must control the contract as much as possible while allowing the client to think he is in control."

"Through flattery and oblations, yes," Freya said. "It was my fault. I showed weakness and he stopped the reading to ask about me."

"Don't worry about it. Small contracts such as this one are good training for you and Stone. Even though a portion of your fee will go to the village, we don't depend on it, so even if you do horribly, you will learn enough to be ready for larger contracts down the road. I wasn't kidding when I told you that I hated negotiations training. I thought it was a total waste of my time and I was right. I never had to sit in on a single negotiation."

"You would have been proud of us, grandfather," Freya said. "We got everything we asked for and more. Mr. Ben even pledged an advance gratuity."

"Good. That will help to ensure additional gratuities later," Sunny Joe said, smiling. "What did you suggest?"

"I asked for monthly deliveries of wild basmati rice," she said.

"Rice? Rice is not a gratuity," Sunny Joe said. "You *buy* rice with your gratuity."

"I don't wear jewelry, and I see no value in silks."

"Your gratuity is up to you," Sunny Joe said. "But remember, you can only negotiate every four years. Is that what you will want four years from now?"

Sunny Joe held up one hand and looked around. Freya froze in place. From his vantage point, Sunny Joe could hear all the regular noises coming from the desert and even a few from some of the nearby houses, but he was more worried about the three heartbeats that had just appeared in the open.

Sunny Joe stood and turned in the same moment.

Freya moved behind him, looking in the direction of her house.

"You better come out while you can still walk," Sunny Joe said. "I don't take kindly to trespassers."

The heartbeats did not match anyone of his tribe. They were slow, methodic, strong pulses that might come from Olympic athletes. Three people walked out from behind Freya's house. The man in front was tall, wearing a tan robe. Freya gasped as she recognized him as the man she had seen in New Orleans. The two girls behind him wore similar robes, though theirs were more femininely decorated with tiny ornate stitching along the edges.

"We mean you no harm," the man said.

"You are trespassing on Sinanju land. Why have you come?" Sunny Joe demanded. He was a bit mad at himself. He should have heard them before they got within fifty feet of him.

"I am Yngvar, imperial attendant for the Lakluun. We have come for the girl," the man said, reaching into his robe.

In the next moment, Sunny Joe was behind Yngvar. After a staccato flurry of movements, the girls were suddenly flat on the ground twenty feet behind them and Yngvar was on his knees. Sunny Joe twisted Yngvar's arm behind his back and took the piece of paper from his hand.

"I deliver a message from the king!" he cried.

Sunny Joe released Yngvar and looked at the paper he was holding. While he had been taught to speak and read dozens of languages, the arcane scribbling on the paper was alien to him. He tossed the note to Freya, keeping his gaze on the strangers.

It had been a long time since she had seen the language, but she was able to read it.

It was the language of her mother.

"What does it say?" Sunny Joe asked, noting the worried look on Freya's face.

"It says, 'The presence of the daughter of the Exile is ordered at the...to the...'"

"To the imperial court of his Majesty Asmund, Monarch of Lakluun," Yngvar said.

"At the King's court to manage the transfer of rights of the Master's Trial to the family of Coh," Freya finished.

"The Master's Trial?" Sunny Joe asked.

"It is a generational challenge," the man in the robe began to say. "We meet..."

"I know what it is," Sunny Joe said. "Each of the Old Tribes sends a representative to combat. Only one survives. I am not familiar with the most recent history, but since the time of Kojong, only the Masters of Sinanju have won."

"Do not make me speak of the Sinanju," Yngvar said, clearly offended.

"Is Freya being called to the Master's Trial?" Sunny Joe asked.

"Of course not," Yngvar said. "Her mother's betrayal has ensured that her descendants can never again participate in the Trial!"

"Then why do you need her?"

"We need Freya to forsake claim to her mother's bloodline before another family can assume the mantle for the next Trial."

"Why would I do you a favor?" Freya said, stepping forward. "You banished my mother from ever returning to her home."

"Then you damn your people for all eternity," Yngvar said, cautiously standing. "Without a representative for the Trial, our people will cease to exist."

"Why?" Freya asked.

"We do not display our skills to the world like the Sinanju," Yngvar said disdainfully. "Our people live to train for the Master's Trial. The representative of one family participates while the rest of the people support the participant. Without the Master's Trial, the very reason for our people's continued existence will disappear."

One of the girls cautiously stepped forward. Her face was veiled, but Freya could tell that they were about the same age.

"If your mother is dead, why have you not returned home?" the girl asked. "Your mother was exiled, not you."

"Why not do it here and get it over with?" Sunny Joe interrupted.

"The ceremony can only be performed on Lakluun soil," Yngvar said firmly. "On the royal grounds."

"Well, you heard her. She's not going," Sunny Joe said.

Freya looked down for a moment. They could not take away her claim to her mother no matter what ceremony they performed.

She had always hoped to return some day, to meet what was left of her mother's family. She knew that now was her chance.

"Wait," Freya said, turning to Yngvar. "How long will the ceremony take?"

"It will take three days to return to Lakluun and a week to prepare for the ceremony, plus your return."

"Are you really thinking of going?" Sunny Joe asked.

"I had planned on returning someday," Freya admitted. "My mother loved Lakluun, but she made me understand that we were no longer welcome there."

"That is not true," the first girl said. "While you may not participate in the Masters' Trial, you are forever a child of Lakluun. Your purple eyes prove it!"

"My eyes are Lakluun, but my heart is Sinanju," Freya said. "That means I must take my responsibilities seriously. Grandfather, with your permission, I will return to the land of my mother."

Sunny Joe thought for a moment, staring into the strangers' faces. He was unable to read the Lakluun people. They were not as strong as the representative they would field at the next Master's Trial, but they had enough training to control their heart rate and other body functions.

Sunny Joe stepped close to Yngvar.

"This girl will be given to your care," he said sternly. "It is your personal responsibility to return her safely. If she is harmed in any way, I'll travel to Lakluun to start the Master's trial prematurely."

"There are no need for threats, Master of Sinanju," Yngvar said. "The Lakluun are a people of honor. If I say she will return safely to you, the entire people of Lakluun will stand behind my word."

"I will need to grab some clothes and—"

"No," Yngvar said. "Your western clothes are not suitable for this ceremony. We will provide for all of your needs. Our people await your immediate return."

Freya turned to Sunny Joe and he saw both sadness and pride in her face.

"Thank you, grandfather," she said. "I will take care of myself."

"I will be here when you return," Sunny Joe said.

Yngvar placed his arm around Freya's shoulder and led her into the darkness. After a few seconds, even Sunny Joe could not see them.

* * *

Sunny Joe sat on the butte, leaning back and gazing up at the silent sky. In this moment of profound stillness, he could feel the vast interconnectedness of life pulsing around him.

The ground under his back was the same Earth that tied all living things together—the same infinitesimal grain of sand hurtling with impossible speed through the same vast and unknowable cosmos.

Life, death, regeneration—a cycle of unique sameness.

The stars wheeling overheard were the same stars that shone on Kojong when he had taken over the Sinanju. The air Sunny Joe tasted was the same air the world shared—but each breath was different from any breath that had ever come before, or that would ever come again. As breathing ceased, lives never truly ended. They just became part of the air breathed by others. Air was a complete history of the world, rewritten anew with every breath.

In that moment, as time and space fell away from him like sand through the fingers of a child, Sunny Joe was whole.

ALSO AVAILABLE:

FORGOTTEN SON

Will Stone and Freya, the lethal brother-sister duo, be enough to help their new boss Benjamin Cole stop the Great Mexican Ninja Army from invading the southwestern United States?
Also available as an audiobook!

THE KILLING FIELDS

Her name is 14. All she really wants is a new best friend…but it's hard to make friends with someone you're trying to kill. Stone and Freya must face off against a bionic killer while inside a nuclear death trap!

OVERLOAD

A figure from Sunny Joe's past seeks revenge by hiring Stone and Freya for a video game where there are no cheat codes…and death is for real!

If you like Jerry's work on Legacy, then you'll love the action and satire of *The Last Witness*!

WARREN MURPHY

WARREN MURPHY was born in Jersey City, where he worked in journalism and politics until launching the Destroyer series with Richard Sapir in 1971. A screenwriter (*Lethal Weapon II, The Eiger Sanction*) as well as a novelist, Murphy's work has won a dozen national awards, including multiple Edgars and Shamuses. He has lectured at many colleges and universities, and is currently offering writing lessons at his website, **WarrenMurphy.com**. A Korean War veteran, some of Murphy's hobbies include golf, mathematics, opera, and investing. He has served on the board of the Mystery Writers of America, and has been a member of the Screenwriters Guild, the Private Eye Writers of America, the International Association of Crime Writers, and the American Crime Writers League. He has five children: Deirdre, Megan, Brian, Ardath, and Devin.

GERALD WELCH

JERRY WELCH is a double-edged threat, both writer and graphic artist. The self-described literary bastard of Warren Murphy and Richard Sapir, Jerry is best known for the writing and artwork in his "Last Witness" series. **www.TheLastWitness.com**

Jerry prefers to be known as one of only four people on Earth ever to be granted the title "Honorary Master of Sinanju."

His personal website is **www.JerryWelch.com** where he's always blogging about something or other.

"I AM CREATED SHIVA, THE DESTROYER; DEATH, THE SHATTERER OF WORLDS. THE DEAD NIGHT TIGER MADE WHOLE BY THE MASTER OF SINANJU. WHO IS THIS DOG MEAT THAT DARES CHALLENGE ME?"

CPSIA information can be obtained at www.ICGtesting.com
Printed in the USA
LVOW06s0219060215

425954LV00029B/669/P